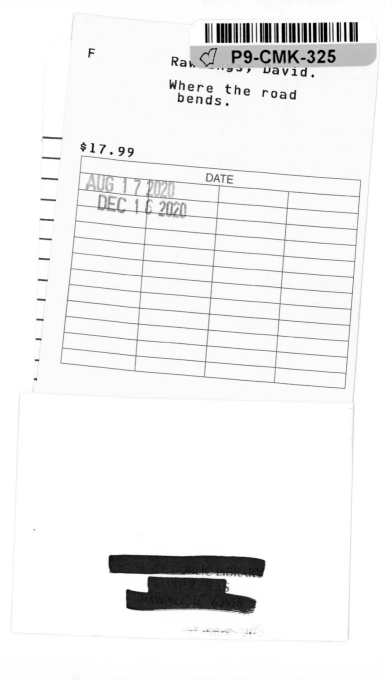

F

Rawlings, David.

Where the road bends.

$17.99

ACCLAIM FOR DAVID RAWLINGS

Where the Road Bends

"What happens when the past collides with the future? In *Where the Road Bends* Australian novelist David Rawlings opens the window of the soul and draws the reader into the lives of characters thrust into the hostile, unknown world of the Australian Outback. The way home follows paths unexpected with encounters unforeseen. Begin the journey. And hold on."

—ROBERT WHITLOW, BESTSELLING AUTHOR

"*Where the Road Bends* takes the reader on a familiar journey of past mistakes and future choices. The characters were relatable but flawed with a hope at the end that will inspire anyone who reads this fantastical story. Definitely recommend!"

—MORGAN L. BUSSE, AWARD-WINNING
AUTHOR OF *THE RAVENWOOD SAGA*

"David Rawlings asks good questions. And as you lose yourself in Australia with these characters, you may begin to ask the same questions of your own heart. A writer could hope for nothing better."

—CHRIS FABRY, AWARD-WINNING
AUTHOR AND RADIO HOST

"*Where the Road Bends* is a very well-told story of intertwined lives, and how we learn and grow through caring for others. Engaging and thought-provoking."

—DAVIS BUNN, INTERNATIONAL
BESTSELLING AUTHOR

"In *Where the Road Bends*, David Rawlings has created a mind bender of a story. What exactly happens when four friends get together fifteen years after graduation? Each has something they're running from . . . or is it to? It's in those questions that this book grabs ahold of readers and won't let go. With a feel similar to James Rubart, this book will delight readers who want to think while they read and don't mind a book that twists and turns with a bend or two along the pages. I thoroughly enjoyed the journey and think you will too!"

—CARA PUTMAN, BESTSELLING AND
AWARD-WINNING AUTHOR

The Camera Never Lies

"In his intriguing novel, *The Camera Never Lies*, David Rawlings challenges us to wonder what our photographs would look like if our souls, not our faces, were captured by the lens. This fascinating story will capture your imagination and your heart."

—RACHEL HAUCK, *NEW YORK TIMES*
BESTSELLING AUTHOR OF *THE WEDDING
DRESS* AND *THE MEMORY HOUSE*

"The camera never lies, and neither does this gripping story about unearthing our deepest secrets in the most fantastical of ways. A message relatable to us all, bottled in an adventure we all love to read. Highly recommend!"

—MELISSA FERGUSON, AUTHOR
OF *THE DATING CHARADE*

"A thought-provoking look at the real price that secrets extract—not just from the person keeping them, but from their loved ones too. You'll close this story and be compelled to examine your own life . . . and also look at those around you and wonder, 'Who else looks like they have it all together but is drowning on the inside?'"

—JESSICA KATE, AUTHOR OF
LOVE AND OTHER MISTAKES

The Baggage Handler

"*The Baggage Handler* by David Rawlings is an extraordinary novel that lingered in my heart long after I finished it. Rawlings's fabulous writing highlighted the unusual premise that had me thinking about my own baggage. I want everyone I know to read this!"

—COLLEEN COBLE, *USA TODAY* BESTSELLING
AUTHOR OF *THE HOUSE AT SALTWATER
POINT* AND THE LAVENDER TIDE SERIES

"Throughout the day I found myself itching to get back to this story. You will too. *The Baggage Handler* is a tale that will resonate deeply with those who have held on too tightly, for too long, to the things that hold them captive. That's me. That's you. Pick it up and prepare to have your world turned upside down, then turned right side up."

—JAMES L. RUBART, BESTSELLING
AUTHOR OF *THE MAN HE NEVER WAS*

WHERE THE
ROAD BENDS

Also by David Rawlings

The Camera Never Lies
The Baggage Handler

WHERE THE

THE

a novel

ROAD

BENDS

DAVID RAWLINGS

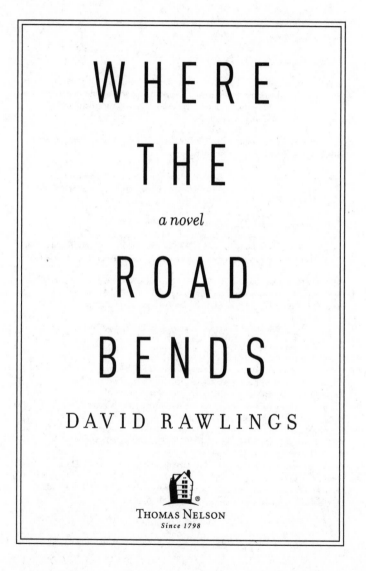

THOMAS NELSON
Since 1798

Published in Nashville, Tennessee, by Thomas Nelson. Thomas Nelson is a registered trademark of HarperCollins Christian Publishing, Inc.

Song lyrics from "Beds Are Burning" by Midnight Oil; written by Robert Hirst, Peter Garrett, Peter Gifford, James Moginie, and Martin Rotsey in 1987. Published by Sony/ATV Music Publishing LLC, Downtown Music Publishing.

Song lyrics from "The Gambler," written by Don Schlitz in 1976.

Thomas Nelson titles may be purchased in bulk for educational, business, fund-raising, or sales promotional use. For information, please e-mail SpecialMarkets@ThomasNelson.com.

Library of Congress Cataloging-in-Publication Data

Names: Rawlings, David, 1971- author.
Title: Where the road bends : a novel / David Rawlings.
Description: Nashville, Tennessee : Thomas Nelson, [2020] | Summary: "Fifteen years after their college graduation, four friends reunite, each with their carefully constructed facade. But when they are mystically separated in a sandstorm, they must face what really brought them to this point"-- Provided by publisher.
Identifiers: LCCN 2019054936 (print) | LCCN 2019054937 (ebook) | ISBN 9780785230724 (hardcover) | ISBN 9780785230731 (epub) | ISBN 9780785230748 (audio download)
Classification: LCC PR9619.4.R385 W48 2020 (print) | LCC PR9619.4.R385 (ebook) | DDC 823/.92--dc23
LC record available at https://lccn.loc.gov/2019054936
LC ebook record available at https://lccn.loc.gov/2019054937

Printed in the United States of America

20 21 22 23 24 LSC 10 9 8 7 6 5 4 3 2 1

WHERE THE
ROAD BENDS

PROLOGUE

Fifteen Years Ago

The four mortarboard tassels flicked away the past and ushered in the future as they arced in the afternoon sun. The circle of friendship that withstood four hard years started its inevitable loosening; the glue that bonded their foursome eased away as the cheers across the quad died away. The clock started a lifetime of mesmeric ticking, a time for potential to become performance.

The first hand thrust the caught cap onto a head of bouncing red curls. Bree Carter choked back tears as she flicked the tassel from her eyes. "I can't believe it's all over."

Andy Summers grabbed his mortarboard and spun it between his fingers, his lithe forearm muscles rippling as the billowing gown's sleeves fell away. "This moment has been so far away for years and now that it's here, it doesn't seem real."

Another hand snatched a graduation cap destined to fall

onto the head of a stunning young woman with jet-black locks. Eliza Williams. "I know, Breezy. It's hard to believe we're finished, but now the next chapter of our lives begins."

Lincoln Horne casually swung his graduation cap by its tassel. A perfect smile beamed from under contoured, don't-care rusted-blond hair. "And I can't wait for that next chapter to start." He gave a cheeky wink to Eliza.

Bree wiped away a runaway tear. "I'm not ready. I'm happy enough to stay here."

Andy smirked at Bree. "Out of the four of us, you're probably the one with the least to worry about. An audition in New York and the chance to record your own CD? I just hope you remember us when you make it big!"

Bree bit a quivering bottom lip. "I don't know . . . It's a long way to go for a long shot. What if I fail?"

Eliza scolded her roommate with a waggling finger, an action she'd perfected in their dorm room. A replacement mom without the undercurrent of guilt. "It's your chance to prove everyone back home wrong."

Andy threw an arm around Bree's shoulders. "I believe in you. If I didn't I wouldn't have lent you the money to go. I want to help you achieve your dream, and now that I've come into some money, I can."

Lincoln bowed theatrically to the group. "No need to thank me again for the tip, Mr. Summers. I thought you'd like to know our star player would be a last-minute withdrawal against Clarendon University. No one else knew, so I'm glad you acted on my advice."

Andy beamed. "It started the biggest lucky streak ever! Long may it continue. I'll be a millionaire before I'm thirty."

Lincoln placed a firm hand on Andy's shoulder. "Slow down, buddy. I've told you a thousand times before. Life is more than what we earn; it's the good we do with it."

Andy bowed his head in deference. "Thank you, Brother Horne."

Eliza's black hair swayed as she tut-tutted, back in her familiar den mother role. "I told you to be careful, Andy. You don't want to head down that road."

"What road? You have to live a little, Lize. Anyway, when you're a huge name, Breezy, I know you'll pay me back with front-row tickets for life."

They shared a laugh, the common soundtrack to life at college. Except this time it petered out, almost as if the soundtrack was entering its coda.

Bree's tears returned. "So when do you leave, Linc?"

Lincoln's enthusiasm bounded into the conversation. "Eliza and I leave in two weeks. I can't wait to start building the school in Uganda. Now that graduation is out of the way, we can really focus on changing the world, you know? And I've got a big surprise planned for us."

Bree patted Lincoln's arm with a quizzical glare at Eliza, who rejected her plea with the tiniest shake of her head.

A frown cut through Lincoln's wide-eyed innocence. "What?"

Eliza crinkled her nose. "I need to postpone the Africa trip for a while."

Lincoln's mouth dropped open, and Bree squeezed his waist.

"Something's come up—an internship in fashion—and it just feels like the smart move is to take it. Maybe we can talk about going out and changing the world after that's over."

Lincoln's grin slid from his face as he folded his muscular arms. "When did this come up?"

Eliza looked away at the dispersing crowd as Andy nudged her. "Good for you, Lize. I'm so proud of you."

A thin smile settled on Eliza's face as she studied the ground. "Thanks, Andy, you're a pal."

Silence descended on the foursome—unheard of in the nonstop chatter since that chance grouping in their first anthropology project in Professor Snowden's classroom and cemented in mind-numbing lectures, which had forged a four-year friendship and one romance.

Bree shifted the conversational gears to kickstart the conversation that was grinding to a halt. "You guys have gotten me through college. That won't stop, will it?"

Eliza left Lincoln's brow-knotted grimace unreturned. "Of course not. Let's just enjoy the moment. Aren't we celebrating at Andy's place?"

Andy grinned. "It will be my pleasure to host my favorite Flagstaff College alumni with all the food and drink money can buy, courtesy of the little birdie Lincoln knows inside our basketball program."

Bree frowned at Eliza. "How will we make sure we won't drift apart?"

"We'll make it work. We don't have to be in each other's pockets to still be in each other's lives. Enjoy the opportunity in New York."

Andy smoothed his oversized gown. "If Bree's worried we'll lose touch—and I don't think she has any reason to be—let's put something in place to catch up in what . . . ten, fifteen years? We can share our stories of greatness and how we got there."

Bree wiped away another tear. "What, like a dinner?"

Andy guffawed. "A dinner? You'll be a famous musician by then, so you can pay for us all to travel to the other side of the world!"

Bree waved off Andy's enthusiasm, which only drew another finger waggle from Eliza. "You won't get that recording contract if you don't start believing in yourself."

Lincoln leveled a pleading look at Eliza, who mouthed back, *Not now.*

Andy snapped his fingers. "Why don't we go back to the beginning? In that very first project in anthropology class, we studied outback Australia. What do you think about heading there?"

Bree shuddered. "All those spiders and snakes? Are you sure it will be safe?"

"You're presuming we'll survive the next fifteen years." Andy thrust his hand to the middle of their circle. "So what do you say? Who's in?"

Bree's smile emerged through the tears as she placed her hand on top, followed by Eliza's. Lincoln's hand was the last to join, his brow furrowed as he failed to catch Eliza's eye.

Eliza looked around the circle with a frown. "Fifteen years! That's our thirties. Middle age! That's so far into the future."

Lincoln forced a smile. "So was graduation."

Bree folded her arms, pinning down her gown now billowing in the growing warmth of the afternoon breeze. "Can you imagine what we'll look like?"

Andy cackled. "I'll bet you one thing. If Bree hasn't conquered the world, I'll be the most successful."

Bree slapped the mortarboard from Andy's hand. "Dean Fulwood talked about not getting ahead of ourselves on the road of life, but to enjoy the journey."

Eliza stared beyond the group, wistfulness softening her expression. "He could find a way to jam that marketing slogan into anything."

Andy threw his arms wide, drawing them into the close circle they had become. "So I'll see you in Australia in fifteen years. But that's way off. Who's up for a party?"

ONE

Present Day

With the gloss of their fifteen-year reunion fading, the buzz of excitement settled into the sharp ache of anxiety. One set of American thumbs twiddled on the cold gray table in the interview room of a police station parked in the red dust of the tiny town nestled in the heart of Australia. Fingernails of a second tourist beat an impatient tattoo, while another set of American nails was already halfway chewed away.

The ordeal started long before the police car ride back into civilization, the unexpected bookend to a reunion that had started days earlier. Their story—which they each thought to be unbelievable—turned out to be a variation of someone else's. Except one, which went unspoken. That someone else should have been sitting in the empty chair, but the police had found no trace at all, save for a neat stack of rocks at their campsite.

There was no question they would stay around—the police were not keen on them leaving—but there was no way they could leave one of their group behind. Silence fell on the windowless, white-walled room, punctuated by drumming fingernails.

A hard swallow and a jerked thumb toward the closed door. "How can we explain it to them?"

The fingernails stopped in midtap. "It has to be the tour group. I can't think of how else to explain it."

A shake of the head and a lowering of bitten nails. "At least you two didn't have to run for your life."

A quiet voice, buried deep in thought, said, "Still, there's a part of me that's glad I did."

Nodding, the three glanced at the chair where their missing friend should be sitting.

Distant footsteps grew louder in the corridor before they stopped outside their door.

Three heads pivoted. "Do you reckon that's—?"

"It could be that detective. He looked like he doesn't believe us for a second."

Outside the interview room, Detective Green scratched his graying temples as he clutched to his chest a notepad filled with question marks and scrawled, angry arrows. And no answers.

"How do you want to play this?"

Detective Sergeant Winter thumbed through a transcript. "Their individual interviews came up with no red flags. Weird, definitely, but not suspicious."

"Eddie says he's got nothing to do with it, and I tend to believe him."

"What do we do with what they said about their friend?"

The senior detective shook his head. "I don't even know what to make of that or where else to start looking." He turned the door handle.

TWO

Five Days Earlier

Waves of passengers surged back and forth past Bree in an ebbing tide, half happier than her, half more relaxed. From her vantage point behind the tiny square of Laminex that passed for a table at the Rock & Brews café at LAX, it was easy to see who was flying out on their exciting vacation and who was returning to the every day, their expressions already recoiling under tension.

Bree's fingers toyed with the apple she'd bought with reluctance. The money from Sam's extra shifts at the nursing home would fly her to Australia, fulfilling a promise made in another time by another Bree, but their straining family budget hadn't stretched to the pricier snacks on the menu. Overpriced fruit it had to be.

Another time. Before Sam and his belief in her—a salve

for the wound to her self-esteem, opened around the kitchen table of her childhood. An easy target for a wounded sniper. Before the girls and their love of music. She was glad to have passed that on and hoped she could guide them to avoid the same mistakes she'd made.

Time ticked on, a slow drip after the flooding rush of a race to the airport and boarding a flight among family tears, most of them hers.

Bree stared at the musicians whose photographs paraded on the café's signage. McCartney and Lennon. Jagger. Springsteen. Musicians she'd hoped to join in the future of her past, but they weren't in her present. The bitter pang of disappointment bit down on her hard. Bree used to hope her music would make a big splash. But after floating for years, she felt like she'd never even made a ripple. And she was still paddling in her small pond.

She banished the creeping negativity with a practiced hand and summoned back the excitement that had warmed her the minute the plane had pushed back from the gate in Nashville, the space around her quiet, free from demands. A space of her own.

A chunky guitar riff drifted across her table, followed by an angel voice Bree knew had been crafted by a sound engineer in a cramped, smoky studio like the one in which she worked on the wrong side of the mixing desk. The TV screens filled with the latest sneering teen sensation, delivering a song written by someone with real talent. Someone like she used to be.

Bree checked her phone. They'd be boarding their flight to Sydney in just over an hour. Where were they all? She tried Eliza's cell phone again with no success.

Bree turned over the apple in her fingers. Ten days in the heart of Australia with old friends. She smiled at the memory of Sam's reassurance as she boarded her LA flight.

"Look, maybe you aren't the person you used to be—who is?—so take some time away to rediscover that. Forget about the three of us and fulfill the promise you made to your friends. Once again, Breezy, you are completely overthinking it."

She was lucky to have Sam, a man happy for her to reconnect with old friends while he guarded their princesses—in an age where some of her girlfriends seemed to use their weekly coffee date to moan about men making their lives a misery. Self-doubt threatened to engulf her without her white knight by her side.

This trip was more than fulfilling a promise. It was the reporting back of what they'd done and who they'd become. At graduation it was all about unfulfilled potential. Fifteen years down the track, it felt a lot like regret.

The outgoing crowd parted like the Red Sea for a tall, elegant woman, somehow separate from the crowd while immersed in it, wearing large sunglasses pinning down jet-black hair at her crown. Bree breathed easier as she waved. Recognition eased across Eliza's face, and she nudged her way through the traffic, her smile on high beam.

Eliza hadn't aged a day since graduation. Following her rise through the ranks of fashion glitterati from the comfortable sidelines of social media warmed Bree's heart but had frozen her self-confidence. Her old friend had everything—the looks, the figure, the apartment, and the high-powered job.

Eliza enveloped Bree in an embrace, and the diamond eagle on Eliza's jacket scratched her nose. "Breezy, it's so good to see you." As Eliza stood back and held her by the shoulders, Bree felt a foot smaller and thirty pounds heavier in her old friend's shadow. Her own red hair had been her greatest asset in college. Now it wasn't quite a liability, but it had slid down her balance sheet.

"Where are the guys?"

Bree shrugged. "I can't get hold of Lincoln."

"Shall we head to the gate and wait for them there?" Eliza turned and carved a wake as they pushed upstream against the tide of traveling humanity. Bree fell into line with Eliza's long stride, skipping on the occasional step to keep up with leopard-skin luggage.

Eliza slowed. "I'm so glad you decided to take advantage of Sam looking after the girls. You don't know how lucky you are—the girls in my Pilates class don't think he's real."

Bree chuckled. "Just lucky, I guess. Did you enjoy the show in Miami?"

Eliza nodded. "It was all right. It was good to see some sun again and get out of the cold for a while."

"But didn't you win a big award?"

Eliza powered through the crowd. "They give those things out like candy, so it was just my turn. Anyway, did Emily's concert go well? I saw the photos you posted."

Bree skirted a family parked in the middle of the walkway, juggling climbing children and a mountain of baggage. "She loved it, but a recital is a recital—five minutes of interest in a two-hour program. Oh, before I forget—" Bree rummaged through her handbag and drew out a small bracelet of painted pink-and-yellow beads and twine, shining with glitter. "Emily made this for her auntie Lize."

Eliza slipped the bracelet over her wrist. "You tell her Auntie Lize loves it and I'll wear it in Australia. How are Imogen's singing lessons coming along?"

The crowd thinned as they approached gate 58. Bree and Eliza batted back the focus of their conversation to each other like Wimbledon finalists as they found two empty seats next to the window.

Eliza scanned the crowd for familiar faces. "We're doing it again, aren't we? Trying to downplay the successes in our lives."

"I guess it's what we do. You're glad I'm taking time off from the family, and I'm glad you could fit this trip in with your busy schedule." Bree squeezed Eliza's knee. "I'm so glad you came."

"I couldn't leave you on your own and a promise is a promise, isn't it? Plus, this trip has come at a good time, to be honest."

"What do you mean by that?"

Eliza pursed thin lips. "The chairman has asked me to consider the CEO job."

"So you'll be running your own fashion label? That's amazing!"

Eliza's face showed she didn't share Bree's excitement. "You'd think so, wouldn't you? I'm one step from the pinnacle of my industry, but something isn't sitting right. Going to the middle of nowhere and dropping offline is exactly what I need at the moment. And I've been researching it. Did you know there's an outback thing in Australia called a walkabout? Although I read somewhere they don't call it that anymore. A journey of self-discovery—maybe I could do something like that. Find out what I'm supposed to be doing in life."

"But you've got the perfect life. Aren't you happy?"

Eliza gave the tiniest shake of her head as she continued scanning the crowd. "I feel like I'm supposed to do something different, you know? Something that means something—"

"But you're so successful." Bree couldn't comprehend her friend's perfect life being anything but a dream. "Unless this is about something else?"

Eliza rolled her eyes. "I hope you're not referring to having a man in my life. I'm above all that biological clock nonsense, and I'm not really looking for Mr. Right, although I sure have dated a few Mr. You'll Dos over the past year. I think it's deeper than that. I thought I'd have changed the world by now."

Bree put an arm around her friend's shoulder. "What did you used to say to me in our dorm? You need to believe in yourself?"

Eliza smiled. "I *do* believe in myself. Maybe I've reached the point where I wonder if I'm believing in the right thing."

"You and I can chat about it under the stars in outback Australia. At least it will be warm for us." Bree surveyed the growing throng at the gate. "So we know Lincoln hasn't changed since college, and do you think Andy has put on even more weight since the ten-year dinner?"

"Who knows? I've spent hours online trying to find him, but even my ninja skills on Google couldn't uncover him. And that cell phone number he gave me at the reunion was disconnected."

Bree leaned into her old friend with a conspiratorial whisper. "Have you worked out how you'll handle Lincoln?"

Eliza shrugged as behind them a plane pushed back from the gate. "There's nothing to handle. Check his social media—he's doing very well for himself and seems like he's enjoying life."

"But what about those LinkedIn notifications you got saying he was looking at your profile?"

"So?"

"Twenty times?"

"It's a free country, Breezy, and he was probably checking my contact details for this trip."

"But twenty times? He hasn't gotten over graduation, has he?"

Eliza laughed it off. "I would *hope* so. We should have all grown up since then."

"Well, on social media it looks like Lincoln is living it up. It's nothing but money and parties."

Eliza frowned. "What did Professor Snowden always say? 'Change is inevitable; growth is optional.' But as I said, that's ancient history."

"Speaking of ancient history—" Bree leaped to her feet and waved at a tall man making his way toward the gate, sunglasses pushed up onto tousled brown hair that looked good despite the late hour. He wore a faded Switchfoot T-shirt under a linen jacket and chinos. "Linc!"

He beelined toward them, a huge smile splitting his face. Bree rushed to throw her arms around him. "I'm so glad to see you."

"You too, Breezy. It's hard to believe that the last time the three of us were together was fifteen years ago. It feels like yesterday."

A heady cloud of cologne enveloped Bree as she shot a raised-eyebrow look at Eliza, before she gazed back into a familiar face that could have been lifted from their yearbook photo. He hadn't aged a day either. She hoped Andy had been battered by storms in life similar to hers, if only so she could share the tag of ugly duckling. "You didn't come to the ten-year dinner."

Passengers milled around the gate as a shadow passed over Lincoln's face. "Work was crazy so I couldn't fly in. We've got this ridiculously long flight to catch up on all that anyway." He peered past Bree. "Hey, Lize. Is it okay to still call you Lize or is Mrs. . . ."

Eliza stepped forward, and Bree clocked the smallest hesitation before their polite embrace. "Lize is fine."

Bree stood dwarfed between two old friends who could easily have passed for runway models. Still.

Lincoln surveyed the growing crowd. "Andy not here yet?"

Eliza checked her phone. "No, and I couldn't find him online either. How can you do business in the twenty-first century without being online?"

Lincoln scrolled through his phone. "I need to see the airline." He charged off to a counter staffed by a flight attendant in a green-and-yellow uniform.

Bree grinned at Eliza. "Feels like yesterday, eh?"

Eliza's jaw clenched. "Ancient history."

Lincoln returned, his cell phone to his ear. "Do you remember what Andy was like in our early conversations?

Couldn't wait to get away on this trip, but since a month ago we've heard nothing, apart from one message asking me to lend him the money for his ticket." He lowered the phone. "Voice mail." He pulled back his sleeve and checked a glittering, chunky Rolex for a moment too long, as if giving it its moment in the spotlight. "We board in fifty minutes."

Eliza smirked. "When was Andy ever quiet about anything?"

Bree's gaze was drawn to Lincoln's wrist and she whistled. "That looks expensive."

"When you're in stockbroking, it's important to wear your success." Lincoln glanced at Eliza's wrist. "Good to see you're doing it, too, Lize."

Bree elbowed Lincoln. "That was a gift from my girls. Hey, didn't you bring home a bracelet from that African orphanage you went to after graduation?" Another quick-fire glance at her old friend.

Lincoln shuffled on his feet, a hardness swirling across his face. "Probably." He studied the incoming passengers as he rose on his toes. "If Andy doesn't turn up, I'll have to get the money from him somehow, but I don't really know how. It's like he's disappeared."

THREE

"*Pacific Australia flight 8779 will be boarding shortly.*"

Lincoln's blood pressure thumped in his ears with each unfamiliar face that joined the massing throng at gate 58. Heads down over phones—sharing the excitement of impending travel with the remote masses of social media rather than the living, breathing people within arm's reach.

He turned to Eliza. "I don't even know what Andy looks like now."

"You would if you had come to the ten-year dinner. He was a lot quieter than he used to be and he'd put on some weight, but haven't we all?"

A bitter guffaw burst from Bree before she scrambled for a sheepish shrug. "Sorry."

Lincoln inwardly cursed Andy as he tried the cell phone number he had eventually pried out of him. Voice mail. Again. "So help me, if he doesn't make it . . ."

Eliza's nose crinkled. "While I think it's great you offered, why would you need to pay for him?"

Lincoln looked forward to prying the real answer from Andy. "All he said was things are really tight at the moment. That's fine because I've done really well this year, and I wanted us all to be here."

Eliza put a hand on Lincoln's arm. "If he doesn't make it, I'm happy to help cover costs so you're not out of pocket."

Lincoln smiled down at her hand. "Thanks, I appreciate the gesture."

Bree's foot nudged her carry-on suitcase. "If he misses the flight, I'm sure the three of us can still enjoy the trip without him."

Lincoln again checked his phone. "But I had something special organized."

"It's a lovely thought anyway. How is San Francisco?"

Lincoln's chest puffed as he ran through his honor roll of career achievements. "I won't spoil the story I've got to tell about my success. I took an internship six months after I got back from traveling in Africa and have worked my way up. And the Bay's an amazing place to sail on weekends." His restless glances for Andy grew more frantic. He couldn't miss their flight. The numbers that concerned Lincoln had no dollar signs in front of them—he could cover the cost of Andy's nonappearance with his next stock tip. The number concerning him most was an odd one. Three. Two good

21

friends stuck together like glue and him as the third wheel, making it almost impossible to get Eliza alone.

He exhaled hard. "Bree, I see you're in Nashville. It's great you ended up in Music City. Still playing your guitar?"

Sadness crept across Bree's eyes. "No, not anymore. That dream is long over."

Eliza stepped forward. "But she's got an amazing family— a wonderful husband and gorgeous kids." Yep. Stuck like glue. Andy had about ten minutes before Lincoln would have to rethink his whole plan.

Lincoln chuckled. "Kids, eh? I'm sure you've got dozens of photos to show me on the plane. What about you, Lize?"

"Pacific Australia flight 8779 will be boarding in fifteen minutes."

A thin smile settled on Eliza's face. "Not in the cards for me, but you know what it's like. You just get on with whatever's next." She glanced away, and Lincoln's mind raced. She was unconvincing. *Where was Andy?*

Bree thumbed through her phone. "So what about you, Lincoln?"

Another wave of passengers crested toward them, and it didn't contain a heavier version of his college friend.

"You seem quite popular, as we can all see on social media."

"What is that supposed to—" Lincoln snapped an angry glance back into the furrowed brows of the two women.

Bree raised a hand to her mouth, admonished. "I'm sorry, Lincoln, I didn't mean to pry. It's just that . . ."

Eliza's nose crinkled, and Lincoln's memory fired back to college, and backpedaled from an argument he didn't want to have. Not at the start of a significant trip.

"Lincoln, I insist on paying for Andy's flight if he doesn't make it. It's obviously upsetting you."

Lincoln plastered a wide smile on his face. He had to start this trip on a better foot than this. "Thanks, I'm just tired, I guess. Work's frantic at the moment."

"Well, try to relax. We'll enjoy the trip without Andy."

Lincoln smiled into Eliza's gaze, into eyes he thought he would lose himself in for the rest of his life. But the crinkle above Eliza's nose remained.

Lincoln pulled out his phone, eager for the distraction. He hadn't started well. If this trip went like he planned, he would have to tread more carefully.

Across the concourse, a gate opened, spilling passengers into the airport in a broiling wash of tiredness and excitement, trips ending and beginning. Lincoln scanned the crowd— Andy would be twice as wide as he remembered. There was no one even close to matching that description.

Another check of his phone. Fruitless.

Eliza and Bree thumbed through photographs on Bree's phone, amid giggles he'd last heard at Flagstaff College.

They were as close as they always were.

He needed Andy, and it looked like he wasn't going to show.

FOUR

Andy Summers stared at the drifting landscape miles below as empty country morphed into a patchwork of suburbia. He was lost in his thoughts or, more to the point, trying to lose them.

His generous stomach strained against the seat belt as it dropped with a familiar lurch. His flight commenced its descent into Los Angeles. His clenched knuckles whitened on the armrests, and his stomach growled at the lateness of the hour. There had been no time to grab dinner—not with having to pack everything for a long trip—and he couldn't afford to risk sitting in an airport terminal café while he waited. He had timed his run perfectly and made the flight as the cabin door closed.

It had been a long week. In a long line of long weeks.

Their college pledge—a promise made in the excitement of youth—would pay off in his thirties. A long-term bet that had come good at just the right time. A chance to escape from the month he'd had, the year he'd had, and the people who'd made it that way. And he was pleased Lincoln had covered his part of the costs without asking too many questions, although he needed to ready himself for when they came.

The flight attendant paced down the aisle, reminders about tray tables and seat backs delivered on autopilot. She nodded at Andy's white knuckles. "Nervous flyer, sir?"

Andy gave her a grim smile. It wasn't the flight he was nervous about, nor was it his late arrival that would make his connection to the Sydney flight a heart-pumping race against the boarding call. His nerves were primed for coming back into cell phone range. He fumbled for his phone and tried to switch off an already switched-off device. His stomach rumbled again. "I know we're late coming into LAX. Are you able to check which gate I need for my Sydney flight? And do you have any more peanuts?"

"No to the peanuts, sir, we're about to land, but I can check your gate. Are you flying with us?"

Andy's simple nod shook free a bead of sweat that ran down his forehead and channeled between the jowls rolling out from under his chin. Another lurch. The ground inched closer.

The business-jacketed woman in the aisle seat nodded down at the death grip on Andy's armrest. "You don't fly much?" She offered her hand, a thick gold chain swinging freely under her wrist. "Sue Garland. I'm in telecommunications."

"Andy Summers. I'm a"—he reached for his tried-and-true spiel—"risk management specialist."

"Great to meet you, Andy. Where are you based?"

"Cincinnati." He stared back out the window. Los Angeles and those who wanted to get in touch with him were now several hundred feet closer.

Sue's lean ushered a thick waft of perfume over to Andy. "So, risk management. Who do you work for?"

Andy stared harder out the window. This was where conversations veered toward dangerous territory. He turned to his seatmate with a curt smile. "Myself."

"Great, a freelancer. Going to LA for business or pleasure?"

Relief followed at the neutral question, one that didn't require his answer to be measured for consequences. "I'm heading to Australia with some old college friends."

Catching up with his old college gang was the icing on top of a much-needed cake—the chance to disappear for a while. He hadn't spoken to the girls since the ten-year dinner, but following their online stories from afar had rekindled happier times, memories from an age ago.

"Sounds great! I'm on the way there myself. Who are you flying with?"

Andy hesitated. This answer might require measurement, and he needed to get away from people, not drag them with him.

Sue tightened her seat belt. "Sorry if I'm prying. I thought it might take your mind off the landing."

Andy's stomach growled as it continued its downward lurch, unhappy with a two-minute gorging on the airline's snack, laughingly listed as "dinner." Not for a big guy like him. He turned back to his seatmate. There was so much he wanted to unload, so much that would relieve the pressure if out in the open rather than trapped in a mind revolving in ever-tightening circles. "Thanks, it's . . ."

Sue raised her eyebrows in the uncomfortable silence that settled onto the empty seat between them. But Andy's words wouldn't come—they were well trained to stay where they were.

The eyebrows fell. "It's okay, I used to have an anxiety about flying too. Listen, if you need any help on the flight over, you come and find me and I can help you through it."

The flight attendant leaned across Sue's seat. "Mr. Summers, it looks like we're landing at gate 56 and you'll be boarding at gate 58. You're in luck."

Andy sunk back into his seat. The patchwork of suburbia gave way to skyscrapers and commerce.

That was a nice piece of luck. It had been a long time since he'd had any.

FIVE

Eliza studied Lincoln over the top of her cell phone, as she fired off her final emails before boarding. For a guy seemingly happy to splash money around on cars and sailboats, he was too invested in losing the money he'd lent to Andy. But the bigger thought was both a worry and a relief. The man who'd snapped at Bree was no longer the compassionate idealist who was generous to a fault.

"Pacific Australia flight 8779 will be boarding in ten minutes."

Lincoln angrily pocketed his phone with a huff. He glanced into Eliza's gaze before plastering another false smile over it in a hurry. That was the relief. Her gut was right back in college. He wasn't the right man for her, and Africa wasn't the right place either.

Two gates away, a crowd trickled from the Jetway. First came the business suits and expensive smart casuals. Then singles and couples without children strolled off the flight without a care in the world. The crowd poured out as economy took its turn to empty: tall, short, fat, and thin. The everyone else of travel. Among the crowd, a disheveled man pushed his way into the airport, his portliness straining a creased dress shirt at the buttons. Thin wisps of sooty hair poked out from under a battered fedora as the man frantically scanned the boarding queue at gate 58.

Eliza nudged Lincoln and pointed. "You can relax about your money now."

The man who looked like he needed a good wash and iron had filled out further since the ten-year reunion dinner.

Lincoln raised a hand and whistled. "Andy!"

The disheveled man acknowledged the wave with a tired smile and made his way over to them, dragging his oversized, bulging suitcase, and his smile broadened. "My favorite Flagstaff College alumni. I can't believe I made it."

Bree pushed aside his offered hand and embraced him. "You always did cut things close."

Andy laughed it off, but it looked like his eyes hadn't gotten the memo to join in. He stood back from Eliza. "You look amazing, Lize." He quickly moved toward her. "I'm sorry, I hope you're not offended by that and it's okay for me to—"

Eliza dismissed his apology with a kiss on each cheek. "Not at all. I didn't think you were going to make it.

Lincoln was freaking out that he would have to chase you for money."

Lincoln pulled him into a backslapping man-hug. "So glad you could make it, man! You really were cutting it fine." He raised a hand to the flight attendant behind the counter. "Now that we're all together, I've got a surprise. I've arranged upgrades for us all at the gate." Bree squealed as Eliza smiled. So that's what he was angry about. Still . . .

"I wanted to mark our reunion with something special. When I get back, I'm going to be made a partner in my stock-broking firm, so it's the least I can do."

Bree's eyes welled. "Lincoln, you don't have to—"

"But I want to. Think of it like Andy helping Bree get to her audition in New York."

Eliza again put her hand on his arm. "That's a lovely gesture, thank you." Bree winced, and Eliza shook her head. Bree's audition might have been fifteen years ago, but clearly the nerve was still raw. Lincoln led them to the counter and handed over their boarding passes with a beaming smile.

Lincoln turned to Andy. "You're a hard man to track down."

Andy scuffed the floor with the toe of his dirty Converse sneaker. "What makes you say that?"

"The fact you aren't on social media and you never answer your cell. Where have you been hiding all this time?"

Andy's eyes narrowed. "Chicago."

A point of connection. Eliza stepped forward for her up-graded boarding. "I've got family in Buffalo Grove. Where are you working?"

Andy's fingers fumbled his new boarding pass. Eliza had seen enough fidgeting from colleagues hemmed in by the final sweat-extracting days of a financial quarter to recognize a drug habit when he saw one.

"I'm working in sports . . ."

Eliza leaned into him. "Fantastic! Bears? Blackhawks? White Sox?"

Andy's fingers kept fidgeting, a man obviously keen to shut down this conversation. "A bit of each, Lize. I'm a consultant." He yawned with an extravagant stretch, his jowls wobbling.

Lincoln elbowed him. "Playing hard to get, hey, buddy? That's okay. We've got a long flight over and ten days to catch up."

"Yeah, sure." Andy's gaze flitted around the gate as if to completely contradict his words.

"Pacific Australia flight 8779 welcomes all passengers to our flight to Sydney, Australia. We welcome those in first and business class to board now."

Lincoln reached for his suitcase. "That's us. Let's get this reunion kick-started, eh?" He lowered his upper body in a deep bow, ushering the others to join the queue.

Bree scanned her boarding pass and waited for Lincoln

before they strolled down the Jetway, anticipation of the Holy Grail of business class bubbling with each step.

Eliza made way for Andy as the queue inched forward and another flight attendant in a green-and-yellow uniform held out her hand. "Your boarding pass, sir?"

Andy handed it over and waited for her at the entrance to the Jetway, but he looked beyond her, frowning at the crowds in the airport. Eliza placed a hand on his back. "Looking for someone?"

Andy snapped out of his daydream. "No. It might be the last trip I go on for a while, so I'm taking it in."

Eliza threw an arm around Andy's shoulder—which took more of her arm than it used to. "Lincoln told me you needed to borrow some money to come with us, so I just wanted to say thank you for still coming. It must be hard. Listen, we're flying back through here, so it's not like this is the last time you'll see LA. Why don't we talk on the plane about how we can get you back on your feet and back to where you were?"

Andy grunted under his breath as he shuffled down the Jetway. Eliza was sure she heard that Andy didn't want to go back there.

SIX

Their circle of friendship closed back into shape more with a slide than a snap; fifteen years on from a lost connection past and forty thousand feet above the Pacific.

Lincoln raised his glass to the curved, shuddering ceiling as he rode minor turbulence on the balls of his feet. "To our graduating class and the chance brilliance of Professor Snowden for introducing us in anthropology. To our combined success and rekindling old friendships!"

Lincoln clocked a knowing glance between Bree and Eliza as they reclined in business class luxury. Andy leaned against their seats as Eliza gripped her orange juice. "Not joining us for a toast, Lize?"

"This will do."

Glasses clinked, a starting bell for the rush of memories. Bree was first out of the blocks. "Do you remember when the fire alarm went off in the middle of our second-year exams?

Lincoln convinced the dean that not only did we need to take the exam again, but we needed different questions as we'd already seen these ones."

Andy chuckled as he drained his glass. "What about the lecture rooms in the Schultz building? I can still feel that hard plastic cutting my back in half."

Bree talked through an extravagant yawn. "The metallic ticking of that clock will never leave me. Remember how its tempo slowed the longer the lecture went?"

The laughs flowed as the years peeled away, and the foursome slipped back into their old friendship, transported back to a time before the comparison trap of social media, adult responsibilities, and extra pounds.

Lincoln leaned against a seat. Eliza had hardly changed much in fifteen years. "I've got no idea how you loved that anthropology class. Professor Snowden put me to sleep."

Bree laughed. "Oh man, she was something else. Do you remember that girl who actually fell asleep ten minutes into every lecture for that entire semester? Kelly something. Whatever happened to her?"

Eliza sipped at her juice, her nose crinkling in the same way it used to in college. The way that would drive Lincoln insane and weak in the knees. "She married some hotshot counselor who wrote a best seller."

Andy flagged down the flight attendant for a refill. Lincoln's curiosity needed satisfaction—he needed to chip away at Andy's mystery, and he wanted to fill in the blanks of the lives Bree and Eliza presented to a social media world. Bree's lack of music. Eliza's lack of a partner. But Andy's story since college was blank. He had to know. "Do you remember at graduation when a certain Mr. Summers bet he would be the biggest success in our little group? Should we collect on that bet, Andy?"

Andy snapped a look at Lincoln—almost too fast—as if a nerve had been sliced open. Curiosity bit deeper into him. There was more to his story—*that* would be interesting to uncover in the following days.

Eliza cocked an eyebrow. "It's not all about money, you know, Lincoln."

"I know, but how else do we measure how well we're doing?" It was time to play his trump card. "Partner is as high as I can go in my field."

"So you're not into helping people anymore?" Andy's lips didn't quite reach a smile. The thin line seemed more like a sneer.

Eliza raised her juice. "Congratulations! You've obviously worked hard to earn it."

The thunder cleared from Andy's face. "I'm pleased for you."

"Hear, hear!" Bree nodded, then stifled another yawn as she elbowed Eliza.

Lincoln cocked his head. "What?"

"Eliza's got some career news of her own, and it's going to top yours." She nudged Eliza again. "Go on."

Eliza waved her off. "We're talking about Lincoln. Don't steal his moment."

"Well, if you won't, Lize, I will." Bree raised her glass. "To Eliza, who is about to become a corporate CEO."

Andy grabbed a fistful of sandwiches from a passing tray. "Is that Virgo Fashion? It says on LinkedIn you're second in charge."

Lincoln narrowed his eyes. While Andy didn't appear online, he certainly seemed to be lurking in the shadows.

Eliza shrugged. "Virgo's a nice place, and I've done very well in fashion. But . . . I don't know."

Bree tried to pump the energy back into Eliza's achievement. "But you'll be heading up your own fashion label. That's amazing!"

Why was she being so coy about this? The Eliza from college would have been well up for the competition.

Lincoln mirrored her body language and placed a hand on her arm. "Even if you're not that excited, congratulations. So what about the rest of your life? You don't have kids, but what about someone special? Husband? Boyfriend?" He needed confirmation of his suspicions.

She was a stone wall. "No, just me. The planets haven't aligned on that score."

The tiniest spark flared within Lincoln, the torch he'd

not quite snuffed out after graduation. "I look forward to hearing more about that when we're on our tour. Speaking of which, I need to update you on a few things."

Andy's mouth opened to reveal a rolling mix of partly chewed bread, carrot, and sprouts. "Like what?"

"The dangers of Australia. But because you obviously enjoy your food, you need to know about our menu. It probably includes bugs and spiders." He threw a conspiratorial wink to Eliza.

A huge glob of bread and mashed salad fell onto the back of Eliza's seat. Bree nearly dropped her glass.

Lincoln chuckled. "No, really, we'll be in the middle of nowhere for ten days. Totally off grid."

Eliza placed her hand on Lincoln's arm, and the torch sparked again. "That sounds great. I've been researching and I found this idea of a walkabout." She turned to Bree and Andy. "It's a journey of self-discovery and sounds perfect for me. I think I might need to recalibrate."

Lincoln furrowed his brow. "I'm sorry, Lize, I haven't booked anything like that."

"I know, but I could still ask them if I could learn how to do one. I think this trip is going to be significant for me."

A single word landed delightfully in Lincoln's ear. *Significant.*

Andy leaned across their seats, his gaze roaming the iron curtain of business class for more flight attendants. Or food. "What did you mean by the dangers of Australia?"

Lincoln counted the dangers off on his fingers, a recitation he'd memorized to impress recent company over drinks or dinner. "There are spiders the size of your fist, miles and miles of nothing but red desert, prehistoric lizards, and eighteen of the twenty-five most deadly snakes in the world. And if you go hitchhiking along some of their highways, you can disappear into thin air."

Eliza simply laughed as Bree placed her empty glass on a passing tray.

Andy shuddered as he reached for another sandwich. "So what else will we be doing?"

"I emailed that to all of you weeks ago, didn't you get it?"

Andy shrugged.

Lincoln shook his head before he gestured to his seat across the roomy breadth of business class. "I've got all the stuff in my folder. Give me a minute." He strode back to his seat, satisfaction settling on him. The trip was going to be *significant* for Eliza. As he grabbed his leather folder from his armrest, a white envelope fell out and landed on the floor. On it was printed a single word, underlined twice, in familiar handwriting. *Lincoln.*

Lincoln balanced the folder on top of his seat as he picked up the letter and opened it. As the first few words came into focus in eyes now bleary with the fog of lateness and the fizz of champagne, a chill swept across him as his blood seemed to pool in his shoes. He slumped into his seat.

Andy chewed his sandwich, glad for the room to breathe. Lincoln was buried in his reading, a stiffer drink than a celebratory one in hand. "Do you think he was serious about our eating bugs and spiders?"

Eliza laughed. "You'll be fine."

"He doesn't look like he's coming back. I guess he wants to keep it all a surprise."

She turned to him, her brow crinkled. "So, Andy, didn't you get all the information Lincoln sent?"

"I must have missed it." A faint alarm sounded as he sensed an approaching probe. The need to measure his words rose. "Anyway, it will be fun to enjoy Australia with old friends. What are you looking forward to, Bree?"

"All I want to see is a koala. The girls want photos."

"Girls? Hey, good for you. What about you, Lize?"

"I'm eager to drop off the radar. I think I need to find myself."

Andy let out a bitter laugh. "That sounds great, but I don't mind if I'm never found." He winced, wishing he could reel back in regretted honesty. Thankfully the droning of the engines hovered over the place where an uncomfortable silence should have gone.

Bree's brows furrowed. "What does that mean?"

"I'm beyond stressed and need a break, that's all." Andy

had to move the conversation on. "So, Breezy, how is your music going? I know the audition in New York didn't work out, but have you recorded anything?"

A tic pulled at the corner of Bree's forced smile and her slumped shoulders betrayed the bounce in her voice. "Still in Nashville and working for the Rhinestone Recording Studio."

"That's fantastic. So what sort of stuff are you recording?"

Bree's jaw clenched. "Advertising jingles, unfortunately."

"That's okay, you're in the heart of Music City. Do you still pull out the old Gibson guitar to play on Broadway?"

"Not really, I've got two girls now who take up most of my time."

"So you said. Do you have any pictures?"

Bree scrambled in the seat pocket for her phone and thumbed an album into life. She handed it over, displaying a series of toothy and toothless smiles from two young girls in princess dresses and cowboy boots holding an oversized guitar.

Eliza leaned in. "Beautiful girls. Charming little bundles of energy. And very creative, like their momma."

Andy handed back the phone. "Lovely." He looked into Eliza's searching gaze.

"So what about you, Mr. Summers? You said at the airport you're into sports."

A jolt rippled through the plane and Andy reached out a

hand as he fell onto Eliza's seat. He steadied his feet against the turbulence. "Yeah, I'm a consultant. Risk management."

"How long have you been doing that?"

"On and off for a while."

Eliza's eyes narrowed. "Great. It must be exciting to work in sports. What sort of risk management do the Chicago Bulls or Blackhawks need?"

A waft of heavenly cuisine drifted down the aisle, curling its finger to Andy's not-yet-sated hunger. He looked back into the gaze of not one but now two sets of cocked eyebrows.

Eliza spoke for them both. "Is everything okay? Be honest with us."

Another jolt cannoned Andy into the seat across the aisle. A flight attendant dashed toward him as the Fasten Seat Belt light chimed. "Sir, it might be best if you return to your seat."

"Thanks, ma'am, will do." Andy shrugged. "Better go back." He padded down the aisle and buckled in. He let go a huge sigh of relief.

Thank goodness for turbulence.

———

Eliza fastened her seat belt. Across the cabin, Lincoln angrily shuffled papers, a freshly topped-up drink on his tray. He may have won many battles in business in the years since college, but his compassionate nature had been a casualty.

Bree turned to Eliza as she tightened her seat belt. "What do you make of Andy?"

Eliza pursed her lips as the plane shuddered again. "He's definitely hiding something."

"He didn't stay in touch with us after the ten-year dinner, did he?"

Eliza shrugged. "Not really. *We* stayed in touch over the years, but other people don't necessarily need to."

"Or maybe want to? What about Lincoln?"

Eliza exhaled hard. "He's changed. The Lincoln I remember was so excited about helping children in Africa, but he seemed to brush off that memory of it, didn't he?"

"That watch screamed money." Bree wriggled closer, her voice dropping to a whisper. "Do you know the other thing I noticed? No wedding band."

"So?"

"But there was an indentation on his ring finger as if he'd been wearing one."

Eliza studied her old friend. "Will you stop?"

Bree grinned. "Stop what?"

"You know what I'm talking about. We've all moved on since then. We had a thing in college, then I went off to start the rest of my life."

The seat belt warning chimed again, extinguishing its warning light, and the cabin again became a hive of activity. A flight attendant leaned across Eliza, surfing a small jolt as she neatly placed cutlery in front of Bree. "I could get used to this."

The flight attendant unfolded a napkin and swirled it across Bree's lap. "Have you had a chance to look through the menu?"

Bree almost burst out of her seat belt. "I've all but memorized it. To think the girls are probably having grilled cheese. I stocked the freezer so they wouldn't live off it until I got back, and we can't afford for them to live at Jack's Bar-B-Que."

The flight attendant placed a stout wine glass on the tray with a sweet smile. "You have girls? How wonderful. Do you mind if I ask how old they are?"

Eliza settled back in her seat as the gushing conversation about Bree's domestic bliss passed overhead. Was Eliza living in denial of biological clocks and a family who relied on her? When Bree talked about her girls, it was as if she was talking about her reason for living. Perhaps Eliza hadn't found hers yet.

———

Eliza woke refreshed, as if emerging from a warm bath. She stretched in the cabin's half-light and pressed the in-flight entertainment screen into action. Their plane hovered over a sea of black—the middle of the Pacific—but they still had seven hours to go. Australia was a long way away, but this was ridiculous. She'd woken from a good night's sleep, only to find there was enough time for another one.

She settled into the comfort of business class at the start of the break she wanted—no, needed. Not one of those weeks away from work when her email and cell phone kept her on a long-distance tether to the office and problems other people should be handling. No, she needed the type of break where she could disappear for a while; where she could lose track of time and look at a calendar without the faintest idea of what day it was.

Bree breathed deep and soft next to her, getting her wish of uninterrupted sleep. Eliza's eyes adjusted as the information cycled through her screen. Their altitude, their speed. The outside temperature of fifty degrees below zero should she want to step outside for some fresh air. Their tiny plane was stuck on a dead-straight line from Los Angeles to Sydney.

Was she on the wrong course?

Eliza flicked her tablet on and fired open the bookmarked websites she had pored over for a month. The website for Outback Tours sat on top of the rest—and the text that had burned into her soul flared again into view. Text overlaying a photograph of an indigenous man in a black shirt and khaki shorts.

Find yourself in the middle of nowhere.

Those first two words had chipped away at her with infuriating regularity since she'd first laid eyes on the photo. *Find yourself.* The words that had sparked this mini-crisis of self-evaluation.

Eliza had never thought of herself as lost. Since the internship, she had dragged herself up the corporate ladder and around blockages, managing nonperformers, and finding ways not to smash the glass ceiling but slip around it. Relying on herself—a lesson learned in the harsh furnace of business, which burned those around her who were unreliable.

Find.

She stared at the word on the screen. Eliza had spent a month focusing on that word, analyzing everything about herself to find why it annoyed her like a run in her stockings, but now the second word drew her in.

Yourself.

Had she focused on the wrong word? The word *find* had taunted her, poking at her growing discomfort. Maybe it wasn't so much that she was lost but that she was no longer herself. The young woman desperate to change the world had become a passive participant in it, navigating her way through, pressing on but leaving it untouched.

The data of their flight cycled on her screen. Six hours fifty-seven minutes to go. Their tiny plane headed for a bend in the flight path, a change of direction. Eliza zoomed out on the screen. The bend led to another straight line. The plane clung to a predetermined path it couldn't change.

Eliza closed her eyes. Maybe *she* could.

━━━━━

San Francisco shimmered through Lincoln Horne's corner office window. Sweeping views of crystal blue from the Bay Bridge right across to Alcatraz—Angel Island—on a good day. The flags atop the buildings that housed the rest of his competitors in the Financial District fluttered in the shining haze of a lazy August morning. The colors were richer, sharper than normal.

The soft leather squeaked as Lincoln rose on the balls of his feet and smoothed his Brooks Brothers suit pants. A ten-year fight had delivered this stunning water view. It was enough, for the moment. On every drive up to his office, he felt like he'd reached the mountaintop. He nearly had. Two floors away from the summit of his career. In his thirties.

Twenty floors below, an army of employees scurried to work, ready to be told what to do and to think. A shining red-and-green cable car jerked its way through Nob Hill, picking up speed as it threaded its way between the narrow avenue of buildings that shepherded California Street down to the sparkling water.

Lincoln turned at the no-nonsense knock, and the door opened before he could offer an invitation. A silver-haired man in a Gucci suit burst through.

Lincoln hustled around his desk to greet his boss, knocking over an empty photo frame. "Mr. Davidson, come in."

The old man enveloped Lincoln in a solid embrace, slapping his back. "We are looking forward to you joining us on the top floor. You've worked hard and you thoroughly deserve it."

"Thank you, sir. I am definitely looking forward to becoming a partner."

The conversation felt easy, like between old friends more than colleagues. Equals. Lincoln could get used to the perks of a chauffeured limousine and partners-only drinks at The Daily Grill on Geary Street.

Mr. Davidson gave Lincoln a final pat on his back, then headed for the door. He rested his hand on the door handle. "There is one more thing, Linc. You will be sharing an office on the top floor."

Lincoln slumped back on the desk. Everyone had their own corner suite on the top floor. No one shared. What was the point of working like a dog if he had to share the limelight he was due?

Mr. Davidson sneered. "Get used to it. You'll be splitting everything down the middle from now on."

Lincoln woke to the crunchy tinkling of ice splashing across his tray. He reached for the letter and ran his thumb over the gold embossed lawyer's logo at the top.

A letter written on behalf of a wife who was his ex-wife in all but a legal sense.

After all the gifts and all his promises, she'd gone ahead and done it.

＝＝＝＝＝

Bree jolted awake. "Who is it? Emily or Imogen?"

It took her mind a moment to join the rest of her body. Sam wasn't nudging her with one of the girls at their bedside; she was at forty thousand feet, and the jolt was a pocket of colder air. She pushed up the eye mask, cracked open one eye, and looked at the LCD monitor. Five hours to go.

Eliza snored lightly—completely at peace, not a hair out of place even in sleep. The years had been more than kind. They'd been lavish in their generosity.

Bree wriggled her toes, cocooned in warm airline socks. People slept alone in the dim half-light of business class or were bathed in the fierce wash of a screen. Bree needed another nap before they arrived in Australia. Another connecting flight meant she needed as much sleep as possible when she could get it. No different than raising two girls under the age of three.

She lifted a finger to the screen and punched her way through the in-flight entertainment, hoping for good music. She was blessed—the latest album from Dave Rawlings and Gillian Welch. She started the music and closed her eyes. The melodic twang of his guitar. The sweetness of her voice. A rough clipping and tailing of lyrics, somehow carrying both the stab of pain and the promise of hope.

She let her mind drift to the Ryman Auditorium, whose center stage she had once dreamed to grace. She sat, enthralled, at the two voices entwined as one, the song melancholy but strong. What she wanted to be.

The voices rang beyond the final strummed chord, and she opened her eyes, now damp with tears. On the other side of business class, noisy snores erupted from Lincoln—his head thrown back, his mouth wide open as he twitched and rolled in a fitful sleep. Andy was buried under a blanket that twitched with the occasional flicker of obvious dreams.

Bree closed her eyes again and lay her chair fully flat as more melancholy strength piped into her headphones, and her soul. She drifted back to the Ryman and the singular spotlight, under which sat a microphone in its stand, the stage now empty.

———

Andy's fidgeting wasn't driven by a dream. He was trying to escape a nightmare.

With the airline blanket tented over him, he flicked through his tablet, sourcing jobs in Australia, preferably somewhere in the middle of nowhere. Google Maps confirmed

Australia had plenty of that. He had three months on his visa, time enough to work out his next moves.

The blanket dropped away, and Sue—Andy's friend from his Cincinnati flight—looked away from her movie and fixed Andy with a smile. Andy feigned waking from a deep sleep and pulled the blanket back over his head. He had hoped the flight to Australia would be the first time he could stop looking over his shoulder. But the need for a constant state of alertness remained, forty thousand feet above the Pacific.

Andy tapped in Cattle Station Jobs. Months of research revealed that while Texans had ranches, Australians had cattle stations. He flicked through the scant options, checking each one not for salary and conditions but for distance away from civilization.

He selected Onkaparinga Station—twenty-five hundred square kilometers of outback for cattle to roam, which quick mental math converted to about a thousand square miles. About the size of Rhode Island. Surely he could lose himself there for a while. He would draw a line in the sand. Sure, it was another one, but if that line was miles away from the battering waves that usually washed away his good intentions, it would be different this time. It had to be.

━━━━━

The ice clinked in the muted drone of business class as Lincoln reached for the letter. The handwritten wording on the bottom was in the same hand as the front of the envelope.

You shut me out even though you claimed to love me.
Until you get over your past, you will never have a future.
I could put up with it because the money was good, but with all the women . . .

All the women? Hardly. He'd run out of patience explaining he'd stayed faithful to his marriage vows while it became obvious she had no intention of keeping hers. The "other women" had only started once Dianne had kicked him to the curb, saying she didn't want him back under any circumstances. She'd only gotten back in touch with him once news spread that he would make partner.

She'd added one last line to her own note at the bottom. In defiance. To make an angry point.

"And it's because of this mental anguish that I want more than half."

Mental anguish? Their marriage had crammed two months of his happiness into two years. *Two years!* His head pounded as the alcohol fought with his broiling anger. Lincoln chugged the rest of his drink, drowning out the anxiety that threatened to overtake the excitement of the reunion.

He scanned the legalese dotted throughout the letter, his

thumb brushing over the embossed lawyer's logo at the top of the page. *Formal notice of intention . . . file for divorce . . . irreparable differences . . . division at the court's discretion . . .*

But he drew his gaze back to her words that cut him to the heart: "Until you get over your past, you will never have a future." Lincoln was tired of hearing that, and it came from more sources than Dianne.

He dragged his bleary eyes to the far side of the cabin. His past was fast asleep. He flexed his jaw as his determination to reconnect solidified in his vodka-soaked, sleep-starved mind.

━━━━━

Bree sat in the center wedge of a packed auditorium, hemmed in by a murmur of impatience. The stage was clear, a single spotlight pinpointing a Gibson guitar behind a single microphone on a stand. The audience waited on tenterhooks for the next act to arrive.

The impatience grew as Bree craned her neck to see into the wings of the stage. Who was due to perform? She wracked her brain—she didn't even know who she was here to see.

Bree felt eyes on her. To her right, a woman in gray drilled her gaze into Bree. Beyond her, a balding, ruddy-faced man in a checked shirt glared. She again scanned the empty stage for some clues—any clues—of who was due on the stage and why people were so angry.

Down her row, face after face turned to her, animosity etched into each one. Animosity directed at her.

Why are they looking at me like that?

People from the rows in front of her turned, resting elbows on chair backs, penetrating glares aimed at her. Bree shrunk away from them as the spotlight bounced from the Gibson's neck on the stage. Her thin smile melted into numbing horror at the guitar's pink-and-silver inlay between the frets—frets that had spent years under the flash of her fingers.

The Gibson was hers. Her beloved guitar that had graced the stage and the radio station at Flagstaff College. The guitar she was now using to pass on to her girls her love of music.

A creeping embarrassment heated her cheeks and neck. The entire audience now turned toward her, a few of them jerking their heads to the stage. Anxiety bit deep. Were they waiting for her? There was no way they were all here to listen to her performance.

She fumbled in her pocket for the ticket stub. The dim light revealed the artist's name due to perform. It couldn't be—

A burning spotlight clunked to life from above and illuminated her in her seat. Faces hardened and eyes narrowed as a perfect silence descended onto the auditorium.

They were waiting for her. Ready or not, she had to go up onstage. She felt a tap on her shoulder. Something about the tap felt familiar. Heavy. Accusing. And her mother's perfume drifted across her shoulder.

Gulping down breaths for courage, Bree moved to stand but

her feet remained rooted to the floor. She put all her focus into one leg, but it was frozen. Panic swept over her as she wrenched her legs to move, but she was going nowhere.

From the right wing of the stage, a man emerged, wearing all black and a headset and carrying a clipboard. He moved into the spotlight and leaned into the microphone. "Bree Carter, you're wanted onstage."

Bree was light-headed. There had been a misunderstanding. She wasn't ready to play. Her throat constricted, choking off any words of defense against this wave of expectation she could never fulfill.

The stage manager tapped on the microphone and cleared his throat. "Bree Carter, you're needed on the stage."

Her body refused to cooperate. The spotlight clunked off and the house lights went up. Tut-tuts of disappointment pecked at her shattered confidence as tears flowed and people rose to leave, bitter complaints floating across to her and down to her from above.

The stage manager shook his head. "Sorry, miss, your audition is over."

Over before it had begun. Just like last time.

———

The woman stared back at Eliza from the darkened window, a carpet of blinking Los Angeles lights stretching out behind her. Flawless skin, jet-black hair tied back, two tendrils framing her eyes—chocolate-brown pools of promise.

This woman looked incredible—she *had* to be in an industry with perfection as its prerequisite, creating generations of women with built-in disappointment when that perfect beauty wasn't achieved. Oil to the machine.

Eliza stared into the eyes of her reflection. How did she get here?

At her heart she opposed the ideals she was paid handsomely to champion. Was she that driven in her job that all she did was tick whichever box was next?

Something in the reflection's eyes flickered. A restlessness. A slip of the mask.

With a burst of white light the reflection melted away and Eliza was faced with the harsh reds and oranges of the Australian outback. The rocky ground crunched under her feet as she made her way along a dirt road, emptiness in every direction for miles. She spun, looking for a reference point but was rewarded with nothing.

Ahead of her, the road veered to the left, then sliced toward the horizon. She spun faster. Eliza saw nothing but red, felt nothing but sick. Dizzy and out of control, she put out her arms and a hand reached for her—

She woke with a start, Bree's hand sitting on her shoulder. "We're nearly there, Lize. Sorry to wake you."

Outside Eliza's window the stark black had submitted to the first rays of a sunrise they had spent half a day fleeing. The soft lilac of the sky gave way to the full, rich spectrum of blue.

The flight map said Australia was close. Eliza craned her neck to see ahead of the plane. The first smudge of a haze appeared as an entire continent appeared to rise from the sea. She elbowed Bree and pointed ahead as the exotic, faraway continent came into view and stretched as far as the eye could see. The change was so sudden—like God had reached down and plonked a whole country in the middle of nowhere. Which, in a way, He had.

Bree stifled a yawn. "I can't believe we're nearly there."

Neither could Eliza. She sat back, her nerves still pulsing from the dream. It had to mean something. She had looked into her own eyes and seen something that showed her she needed to change.

Eliza was sure her life was about to restart.

SEVEN

A cramp seized Andy's shoulders as he pulled them in tight, hemmed in by a domestic flight cursed with the lack of the luxurious space of international business class. He had withdrawn into the view. For two hours the ground had changed thirty thousand feet below as the crisscross suburban gray of the city gave way to deep green, which gave way to dusty brown, which gave way to an ochre orange. Now the earth was rich red. It was as if the lifeblood of the country was being cleansed as it flowed back to its heart.

Andy smiled, again safely out of reach. The sign warning against cell phone use in passport control at Sydney Airport had provided him with a welcome alibi. And the adrenaline rush of running the gauntlet of duty-free alcohol had given him a few moments to slip away and buy snacks, security against the possibility Lincoln wasn't joking about eating bugs and spiders.

Andy winced at the only slip—absentmindedly switching on his phone in the airport transfer bus and releasing a cacophony of messages. And while he thought he'd recovered, he was sure Eliza was staring at him from across the aisle.

She leaned across him to see the view. "The outback is huge!" A crinkle appeared above her nose. "We never got around to finishing our conversation from before."

So she had seen it. Andy's defenses dropped into place as he unraveled the spiel the long flight from Los Angeles had allowed him to prepare. "Am I in trouble? I've got troubles like everyone else, and I'm looking forward to unwinding in Australia and getting away for a while, you know?" That answer should withstand serious scrutiny.

Eliza frowned. While his answer might've been perfect, he'd answered the wrong question. "That wasn't what I was referring to."

The familiar chill of uncertainty gripped him.

"You said you never wanted to be found again. What did you mean by that?"

Andy's mind fired in all directions as a new threat found a hole in his carefully constructed perimeter. "I . . ." He slumped with a sigh. He had nothing. "I don't know, what does it mean to you?"

Eliza mirrored his sigh. "You sound like me, that's all. I've had so many demands on me for so long now that I feel the same. There's a part of me that wishes I could disappear too."

Andy's confidence trickled back as a chance to wrestle back the conversation unveiled itself. "Is that why you don't want to take this CEO job?"

"Not really. I'm good enough to do it and do it well. But I wonder if it's the road I should take."

Their conversation found a comfortable groove they'd last hit in college. Andy settled into it, enjoying a connection he'd not felt with anyone in ages.

"We were always alike, and it looks like we still are."

Andy fingered the Mars bar in his pocket. Between the perfect exterior of his friend and his own overweight mess of a facade, he might have found someone who could understand what he needed to do. A realization dawned on him—he still didn't know how he was going to disappear, but maybe Eliza could be an ally.

———

Bree thumbed the video back on for a tenth viewing. Two tiny princesses in cowboy boots shouted into her face. "Good night, Mommy! We hope you see a koala and a kangaroo and we miss you already and wish you were home with us."

Tears welled, as they had each time her daughters yelled their good nights. The video shook and bumped, as it had nine times before, and her screen was filled with Sam's smiling face. "Sorry about that. They didn't stick to the script.

Hope you had a great flight, and if you want to send us a message from Down Under, that would be great. Love you."

Sam froze mid-grin.

Lincoln handed back her phone. "You've got a wonderful family."

"Thanks. I love them more than anything. So what about you?"

Lincoln smirked. "I love them more than anything too."

Bree blushed. "You know what I mean. What about you and family?"

A wary smile surfaced on Lincoln's lips as his gaze darted around the cabin. "I've been unlucky in love, I guess."

"Anyone serious over the years, or have you been playing the field?"

Lincoln exhaled hard. "I've been married."

Wide-eyed, Bree sat back in her seat. "You kept that quiet. There's nothing on your social media that would even hint at that."

Lincoln shrugged. "There's nothing really to share. It was short, and it's over."

"Kids?"

Lincoln looked beyond Bree. "No, it's probably just as well."

"I'm really sorry to hear that. How long—?"

His eyes hardened, lowering a boom on the conversation. "So tell me about your husband. What does Sam do for a living?"

Bree couldn't help but smile as pride in her husband's respectful care of the elderly poured out. Sam's cheeky grin had gotten her attention. His belief in her had won her heart. And his commitment to the people in his care had kept her love burning.

"And you're in Nashville. Still involved in music?"

Bree's red locks shook. "Not really. I work in a studio that records advertising jingles." She bit her lip and looked up at Lincoln from beneath lowered eyelids, expecting to feel his disappointment.

"Well, you're still in music, and I guess if you want to go back to it after your girls have grown up, you're in the right place. Tell me about Eliza."

The speed with which Lincoln shifted the conversation left Bree's head spinning.

"She doesn't have anyone in her life, does she?"

"Why don't you ask her that?"

Lincoln shook his head and beamed a goofy, embarrassed smile. "Didn't we have this discussion in our sophomore year?"

Bree nudged him with a playful elbow. "You want to rekindle something with her, don't you?"

Lincoln's grin slipped.

"You do! Listen, can I give you some advice? I know things didn't end well back in college, but I really think she's moved on."

"It's not that things didn't end well, it's that they didn't end. I came back from Africa and she left me hanging."

An attendant's voice crackled across the intercom. "The captain advises that we'll shortly be commencing our descent. Would the cabin crew please prepare the cabin for landing?"

Bree checked the flight map. Caroline Springs had to be close but it was nowhere in sight. Beneath her, miles and miles of nothingness. Occasional long fingernail scratches in the earth, empty roads ready for the next person who might want to visit whatever was down there, whenever that might be. Maybe the town would appear out of nowhere like Sydney did. Maybe that's what Australia was best at—surprising you when you least expected it.

Lincoln fastened his tray table and adjusted his seat belt.

"That's a shame about your music. Were there any other auditions besides that one in New York?"

Bree could feel herself welling up, as she always did at this part of the memory. She had to keep a lid on her emotions. "No."

Lincoln cocked his head. "Well, you gave it your best shot, didn't you?"

No, she hadn't.

———

Lincoln strutted across the tarmac, his shoulders burning in the lunchtime sun, his heavy eyelids stuck twelve time zones away. He headed toward a colossal corrugated metal building, a sign of welcome nestled in the gentle scooping curve of its roof.

The automatic doors scooched open and Lincoln strode into the crisp coolness of the terminal. He placed his feet on carpet of red ochre with bursts of black and brown. The airport at Coolamon Crossing could have been built off-site and dropped right on top of the outback.

Bree folded back the brim of her wide hat as the cool air buffeted her fringe. "Did you see that giant bird running alongside the runway? Was that an ostrich?"

A woman with chocolate skin and gold flecks in raven-black hair brushed past Bree. "Actually, it's an emu." Her accent was more than flat broadness; its exoticness dripped with dark honey. Her sashaying figure cloaked in a dress patterned in white dots and ochre handprints drew Lincoln's gaze.

Andy appeared at his shoulder. "They don't really care about security here, do they? You could walk to the parking lot right off the plane."

Lincoln scanned for the captivating woman gliding through the airport and jumped as his phone beeped again. Another text from Dianne. The smallest of victories surged through him, and he relished the flourish with which he switched off his phone.

Eliza joined them, her phone swiveling to capture the swirls of color and shape that dotted the walls. "Have a look at the indigenous artwork. Incredible!"

The woman was gone. "Let's head over to baggage claim."

An explosion of messages peppered with an explosion of expletives erupted as Andy fumbled for his phone. Lincoln laughed. "Someone's popular."

Andy mumbled an apology under his breath.

Eliza nudged between them. "I admire your commitment to staying offline, Andy, but it's okay if you answer one message while you're on vacation."

Lincoln turned to Eliza. "Which gate were we at?"

Eliza laughed as she jerked a thumb over her shoulder. "*The* gate."

They approached a single carousel, a thin ribbon of black snaking its way over the ochre and brick-red of the carpet. The carousel creaked into gear and suitcases appeared—black, black, silver, black. Then expensive leather and Lincoln stepped forward. "Mine made it from San Francisco."

A steady stream of luggage filled the carousel and paraded around the tiny airport. Eliza reached for a leopard-print suitcase that dawdled toward them. Andy grabbed a well-traveled canvas. Bree's anxious scanning ended as her suitcase made an appearance.

Lincoln surveyed their group and collective baggage. "Okay, does everyone have everything? If so, let's—"

Andy shook his head. "Still waiting on two more."

Lincoln's eyebrows shot up. "Two more? How long are you staying for?"

Bree sidled up to Lincoln. "Where are we supposed to meet our tour guides?"

Lincoln zipped open his leather folder, and a single sheet of paper, embossed with a lawyer's logo, fluttered to the floor. He bent over and snatched it up, beating Eliza's outstretched hand to it, and shoved the letter to the bottom of his paperwork. His finger trailed down the page as he darted his gaze to Eliza, now engrossed in her phone. "Let's see . . . what am I looking for? 'Our representative will meet you at the airport for a comfortable ride out to our campsite.'"

A flat accent appeared at Lincoln's shoulder. "Sorry to interrupt, mate, but I think that might be referring to me." A young man in a black shirt and khaki shorts stood next to them, a pearly white grin set against jet-black skin and under fine-cropped black hair. Over his heart were two embroidered words: *Outback Tours.* "Are you Lincoln Horne?"

Eliza brushed Lincoln aside as she thrust out her hand. "I recognize you from the website. Eliza Williams."

The young man shook her hand warmly. "Eddie. Eddie McLeod."

Lincoln clapped Eddie on the shoulder. "Great to meet you, bro."

Eddie chuckled. "Sorry, mate. Don't talk like that over here."

Scolded, Lincoln tried to cover his embarrassment by

introducing Bree and Andy as he approached, pushing a cart with three heavy canvas bags threatening to spill from it.

Eddie surveyed the group. "Do we have all four of you? Well, welcome. Let's get started." He turned on his heel and Lincoln fell in behind him, past a colorful display of pink-and-purple paintings made of nothing but dots, baskets of woven grass, and burned wood fashioned into furniture.

Eliza made a beeline to them. "Wonderful! The color, the detail."

Lincoln slowed as they approached the entrance doors to the airport, flanked by two ceiling-high banners, imprinted with photographs of cave paintings—long, sweeping daubs and swirls of ancient art in chalk and red ochre. Shapes that could have been kangaroos and snakes, chased by figures that must have been hunters.

Bree nudged him. "I hope we see some of those while we're in the outback."

The doors slid open and Lincoln was assaulted by a curtain of crisp heat. Head down, a heavyset man shouldered him as he charged past, the corks jumping and swaying from a battered hat; thick, hairy arms jutting out of his dark-blue tank top, straining against the paunch of middle age.

Lincoln stepped around him. "Careful."

Andy wasn't looking. The man charged into his cart, scattering Andy and his bags across the carpet. The man rushed to apologize and picked up his luggage. "Sorry, mate. Didn't mean to bowl you over like that."

Andy brushed himself off and squinted up at the man's outstretched hand. "That's okay, buddy. I should probably watch where I'm headed."

The man tipped his broad hat, the corks bouncing in front of his gleaming eyes. "Shouldn't we all." He burst into a cackle of laughter as he charged deeper into the airport.

"This way, please." Eddie lifted the last of Andy's bags onto his cart and gestured along the curb to a massive black vehicle—the love child of a four-wheel drive and a minibus—parked under metal shade sails embossed with squiggles and swirls. On the side stylized writing matched the embroidery over Eddie's heart: Outback Tours.

The passenger door opened and a second young man in black and khaki jumped out. A crooked grin and a tousled mop of beach-blond hair thrust out a hand. "G'day! Sloaney."

Eddie opened a trailer behind the vehicle and lifted their luggage into it. "Everyone hop in. Let's go explore the heart of Australia."

Lincoln held open the back doors. "Ladies, after you."

Eliza and Bree climbed in with grateful thanks. Lincoln followed Andy into the vehicle and another welcome burst of cool air. The interior was sheer luxury of leather and polish. The seats, padded and tall, would have been at home in business class.

Eddie pulled away from the curb. "We've got a bit of a drive to get out to the campsite. I know you're probably all tired from your long flights, so relax and we'll let you know when we're getting close."

Lincoln leaned his head back against the soft leather and took stock. The reunion had started well. This trip would be significant for Eliza, even if Bree said she'd moved on. Significant could only mean one thing. Him. She was alone and wondering if she'd made the right decision. Perhaps Dianne's letter had come at a good time. He no longer needed to hide a marriage that was dead in all ways but a legal sense. The thread it had hung by for two years was about to be snipped. And it wouldn't get in the way of rekindling an old flame.

Through Lincoln's window the airport disappeared behind them, and the world flattened out. He closed his eyes and listened to the drone of the tires. But not for long.

EIGHT

Eliza's eyelids fluttered open to a red-and-black blur. The red dirt ran parallel to the black asphalt beyond the window that cooled her cheek. She squinted at crisp, white clouds that hung in a sky of azure blue. In every direction was red: the dust powdering the heart of Central Australia and the rocks waiting to be worn down over the next thousand years. The horizon beckoned, a blurred, shimmering, ruled line between red and blue. This was a land of contrast.

Across from her, Lincoln stared out the window. Behind her, Andy and Bree nodded along in the back seat, lost in sleep. Over the tires' drone on the road, a low rumble grew and Eliza looked up into the sky. They must still be near the airport. She tried to shake her head into the right time zone as a tiny, shimmering box grew in the distance, miles ahead on the dead-straight ribbon of asphalt. "What is that?"

Eddie gripped the wheel, the steel sinews in his forearms rippling as if preparing for a collision. "Road train."

"A train? Out here?" Eliza strained to look at the road ahead.

Sloaney threw a comment over his shoulder. "No trains around here for hundreds of kilometers. A road train is a truck. A big one."

Eliza was transfixed as the box grew into a large truck that loomed in front of the window, its bulky red cabin taking up more than its share of the road.

Lincoln whistled. "How big is it?"

Eddie slowed the four-wheel drive and pulled two tires onto the dirt flanking the asphalt. "They don't call it a road *train* for nothing. A big engine pulling along all these trailers."

The road train now filled half the windshield and was almost upon them. Eddie gripped the wheel hard but raised one finger from the steering wheel, as if in greeting. The driver lifted a finger in return, and Eliza swore she could see a rust-red ponytail bouncing behind the cap.

With a thundering roar and a blur of red, the semitrailer rushed past her window, followed by a wall of silvery steel that felt like it lasted for minutes. Their four-wheel drive shuddered as it was drawn into the bouncing wake of the giant truck.

Eddie turned to Sloaney. "That's unusual."

Eliza cleared her throat. "Excuse me? Unusual to see a woman behind the wheel? Isn't that a bit sexist?"

Eddie shrugged. "I meant it's unusual to see a road train this far out."

Lincoln's lips curled in a smirk. "How far have we got to go, guys?"

Eddie tapped his fingers on the wheel. "Not far. Probably another hour?"

"I thought you said it's not far."

Sloaney grinned as he turned to face them. "An hour is a trip around the corner out here."

"How long would it take to drive across the entire country?"

Sloaney's eyes widened as he did the mental math. "Oh, thirty hours—"

Lincoln scoffed. "You can drive from LA to New York in forty."

"—will get you to the red center from Sydney. From there to Perth is another thirty. Nonstop."

Eliza stifled a laugh as she resumed her gaze out the window—the constant red was as bright as in her dream. Now was the time to ask. "So Eddie and Sloaney, I'd love to learn more about the culture, and I'm very interested in doing a walkabout."

Eddie winced as he threw a grim look into the rearview mirror. "I know what you're talking about, but that's not a word we still use, so I'd prefer you didn't out of respect."

Eliza flushed. "I'm so sorry—"

"That's okay, now you know. If you want to learn, then I'll tell you. It's a word based on misunderstanding—it was used to explain something it wasn't, and then painted a picture of people who weren't like that. It was more than just some mythical trek, and it wasn't wandering around on the land as if you were lost. A journey always had a purpose."

Eliza pressed on. "So what was this"—she held back the word that had clearly offended her host and scrambled to find an appropriate one—"journey? It wasn't this idea that you would go into the desert and discover who you are? Being surrounded by your thoughts and being stripped away until you discovered who you are?"

Lincoln sniggered. "I think I went to a Tony Robbins seminar that sounded like that."

Eddie fixed his gaze on her in the mirror. "I'm glad you asked, Eliza. Not enough people do."

"I think it sounds fascinating. I'd like to do one."

Eddie tapped his fingers on the wheel. "Most people tell us that getting away from their mobile phones or their emails for a week is more than enough to refocus."

Surely there had to be more. "Do you have any other traditional ways of finding yourself or discovering who you are?"

Eddie shared a look with Sloaney. "A couple. We can talk about that around the fire if you'd like. The fire is a good place to talk. It brings people together and brings conversations out into the open. And I'd be more than happy to keep talking about the people of the land as much as the land itself."

Good, she could talk further with them, and she would make better use of her time than simply being away from technology. Even if she could learn some techniques, she'd be grateful.

Eliza flicked her gaze from the ruled line between sky and earth to the one separating black road from red earth. The colors melded as her eyelids grew heavier, and thanks to the droning of the tires, she succumbed to her body telling her it was still the middle of the night.

Lincoln riffled through the Australian currency tucked away in his wallet, a rainbow of red, purple, blue, and gold. Such a difference to the greenback. He held a note up to the light. There were even little windows on it, almost as if a helpful country wanted to help you see who was coming to steal your cash. Lincoln turned the bill over in his hand. Unfamiliar faces. A couple of women. "You've got really colorful money. Who are these people, past presidents?"

Sloaney laughed. "We don't do presidents over here. These are famous Aussies." He turned and pointed to the blue note. "The ten-buck note? Banjo Patterson, one of our great poets."

Eddie spoke to Lincoln via the rearview mirror. "The fifty has a black fella on it. David Unaipon. Preacher, author, inventor. Very smart guy."

Lincoln inspected the mustard-colored note. "We have politicians and great leaders on our money. Why don't you have any on yours?"

Sloaney grinned at him, a twinkle in his eye. "The minute we have any, we might do that. Anyway, there's no need for your money out here. Nowhere to spend it. And besides, you've already paid for the trip. So what about you? Married? Kids?"

"Was married."

Sloaney looked first at Eliza, then Bree. "Tough break."

Eliza flinched in her seat. Was she asleep?

Eddie chuckled. "I thought you two must be couples."

Lincoln laughed. "No, old college friends. When we graduated fifteen years ago, we promised we'd reunite and do something special."

"Well, thanks for picking us. You must be pretty good friends to still be in touch all these years later."

"I guess so. Good to see everyone again."

Eddie nodded. "Good man. What do you do?"

Lincoln puffed up as the conversation moved into his wheelhouse. "I'm a stockbroker in San Francisco and about to make partner."

"Good on ya."

A silence settled over the drone of the tires and Lincoln was disappointed at their lack of enthusiasm. "So stockbroking is a trillion-dollar industry of investments in—"

Sloaney raised a hand. "We know. We might live in the middle of nowhere, but we don't live in mud huts. So what do you hope to get out of this trip? Seeing as you're the guy who booked the tour."

"I'm into anything that makes your heart race, so I'm keen to go rock climbing or whatever else you guys do for fun out here."

Eddie winked at him. "We could do that. What about the others?"

"They're up for everything, especially Andy. He's more of an adrenaline junkie than all of us. If you need anyone to hold a snake or chomp down on a scorpion, it's probably him." Andy's generous cheeks wobbled as his face leaned on a folded hoodie against the window. Now that would be funny if it happened.

"Sit back, mate. Not long to go now."

Lincoln leaned his head back, still amused by the surprise Andy was going to get. But a thought shaded his joy—the answer he wanted to give but couldn't in case Eliza was sleeping light. The one thing he hoped to get out of the trip was her.

———

The tires had stopped droning—they now plowed through fine sand as five chestnut and mottled horses trotted alongside their vehicle, weaving in and out of the low bushes. Bree stifled a squeal. "Look! Who owns those horses?"

Eddie flicked wary glances to the thundering herd, his hands jerking the wheel away from their lunges toward their dirt track. "No one. They're brumbies. They're untamed and don't want any kind of help in changing that."

Andy stretched with an extravagant yawn. "Is everything in this country designed to kill you?"

Sloaney laughed. "If you don't have your wits about you."

The flanks rippled on the majestic animals keeping pace with them. Roaming free, manes flowing in the wind, unencumbered by anything. "Where are we?"

Eddie caught Bree's eye. "The middle of nowhere." He slowed the four-wheel drive and the soft shuffle under the tires was replaced by the slow crunch of gravel. The brumbies veered away from this new track as it bent around a clump of low grass and the brakes squealed as they came to a stop. "We're here."

———

The heavy car door creaked open and Andy placed his heels into the middle of nowhere. He felt remarkably refreshed—a sense he hadn't felt in some time. The sun sunk low after a long climb across the sky as the whipping wind buffeted him. How long had they been driving? The terrain was flat as far as his eyes could see, interrupted by small, rocky outcrops—flat stacks of stone slabs teetering as they rose out of the sea of red. God's game of Jenga. The occasional forlorn tree, bent over to the earth, back broken by the weather and the weight of time. Squat bushes punctuated the flat countryside, as if nature itself had given up trying to grow too tall in the harsh Australian outback.

Andy blinked hard and, on autopilot, reached for his phone, before he decided better of it.

Sloaney headed toward the trailer and Andy fell in behind him. "So do we have to put everything up ourselves?"

"Nah, mate. Already done."

Andy spun on his heel. "Where's the campsite?"

Sloaney jerked his head not toward the distance but down. Beyond, a tall, knobbly skyscraper of packed dirt reached majestically into the sky.

Sloaney moved past Andy lugging hefty bags. "Fire ants." Half-a-dozen steps beyond the tower he disappeared—first his legs, then torso, then head. Andy gave the ant construction a wide berth and stood at the lip of a crater. The ground dipped into a circular hollow, fifty yards wide—a giant's thumbprint depression in the earth, dotted with spinifex grass whose sandy-colored, spindly fingers waved against the crater's floor. In the center was a clearing. Seven long, thin tents had been erected around a circle of stones, with dead wood piled high.

A low whistle came from over Andy's shoulder as Lincoln pushed past him and over the crater's lip. "Now this is cool."

Eddie slung a bag from the depths of the trailer. "While we get set up, why don't you choose your swag?"

Andy trod carefully as he entered the crater. "Swag?"

Eddie gestured to the tents as he descended. "Think of it as an outback tent. It won't set any records for glamping, but when the blanket of stars rolls out above you and you can sleep under them all tucked up nice and safe, you'll thank us. No better outback experience than that."

Andy's bulky frame lost consecutive battles with gravity and momentum and with his final steps into the sandy sides of the thumbprint, he ran windmilling into the campsite.

Lincoln peered out from beneath the thin, black mesh of his canvas cocoon. "Good to see you're keen."

Bree whipped out her phone, and obligatory selfies with Eliza were taken in front of their sleeping quarters. "They look like coffins."

Andy ran his hand over the thick, green canvas, taut under the strain of pegs driven into the earth. He peeled back the rough fabric to reveal a thin, black mesh cocooning a mattress, folded blankets, and a rolled-up sleeping bag. The fading blue sky stretched wide above him, soon to be filled with the promise of stars.

Andy circled the floor of the crater, checking for critters. Nothing but dirt and spinifex. He slogged his way through

soft sand as he climbed to the crater's lip, his thighs screaming with the unfamiliar exertion. He pulled himself over the
lip and doubled over to regain his breath in the blustery wind.
Their vehicle was the only sign of civilization anywhere in
this landscape. In the distance graying clouds lit distant hills
in burgundy and purple, and a roiling storm brewed on the
horizon.

Eddie brushed past him. "Are you hungry, mate? Let's
grab some tucker, hey?"

Andy furrowed his brow. "Tucker?"

Eddie's voice echoed from deep within the trailer. "Tucker.
Food. We might have some spiders or bugs you can eat."

Andy froze. He was starving, but there was no way he
would be forced into that. He reached for the softened shape of
the remaining Mars bar in his pocket. He hoped he wouldn't
have to make it last.

Eddie emerged from the trailer, his pearly white grin
beamed through the fading afternoon light. "I thought so.
I'm only winding you up because your mate said you'd be up
for anything."

Lincoln. Andy grunted in frustration. "Are we going to
do anything dangerous?"

Eddie's mouth twisted into a smirk. "We've got some surprises up our sleeves but don't worry, we'll look after ya."

Another flash of lightning, this time closer. "Are we about
to get some rain? I didn't think it rained in the outback."

Eddie shrugged. "We still get rain, just not as often and not as much, but if it does we'll sure know about it."

"Is there any phone coverage out here?"

Eddie shook his head. "Nah, mate. Only our satellite phone. That's what I said to Eliza over there. If you wanted to disappear for a while, this is where you'd go." He shouldered a hefty bag of supplies and disappeared over the crater's edge.

Andy cast a nervous eye toward the bright flashes peppering the hills. He breathed deep as he checked over both shoulders. Alone. He reached into his pocket and held his cell phone aloft, his eyes jammed shut against the messages he was sure he would get. He switched it on, but his phone stayed silent. His eyes drifted to the top corner of the screen. His heart leaped at the two words he desperately wanted to see: *No Service*.

Fourteen messages had flooded his phone when he switched it on at the airport. He thumbed them open and deleted them all, a growing sense of power flushing back through him, a sense of control over his destiny. It had been far too long.

He stared at the landscape and the flashes that were edging closer. They could come as close as they wanted. Those who were after him couldn't.

NINE

The clouds slowly unveiled flecks of silver paint from an artist's wide brush swept across the heavens. A chill moved in as the darkness chased the daylight from the landscape that surrendered by hues—orange to pink, pink to gray, and gray sliding to black. The dried gum tree crackled as the dancing campfire flames consumed it. Shadows shimmered between the swags and the spinifex, and Lincoln was washed in a warm orange glow.

Dirt and ash puffed up from the ground, just beyond the end of the long, thin wooden tube Eddie held to his lips. Guttural sounds pulsed around the crater, a deep drone peppered with staccato birdlike calls. The sound seemed to flow through Eddie from deep within the land, passing through him and giving life to those creatures who lived on it.

Lincoln sat mesmerized as the dying throes of the music landed softly on their campsite, almost like snow, as the silence again engulfed them. "That was amazing. Can I have a try?"

Eddie frowned. "I've got permission to play this yidaki,

and I do pay my respects to the Yolngu people of the Top End when I play it."

Eliza leaned into the circle of light. "What a wonderful instrument that symbolizes your people. Do all Aboriginal people learn to play the didgeridoo when they're young?"

Eddie chuckled as he rolled the instrument in his hands. Its pattern of fine white dots and brushstrokes fired in the firelight. "Another piece of culture for you to learn, Eliza. Like I said, this is a yidaki and not everyone plays one, but I do like playing it out here."

Lincoln smiled as Eliza backed away from another cultural gaffe. She was still the headstrong go-getter whose feet could alternate between her mouth and backpedaling from offense.

"Still, it is a wonderful example of an ancient culture. You really do evoke a rich history developed over thousands of years."

A metallic, shrill chirping knifed through the silence. Eddie reached for his pocket and looked at the screen of his satellite phone with a wince. "Sorry, it's my auntie. Always checks up on me." He stood and walked into the darkness. "Auntie Deanne. No, we're okay . . ."

Lincoln scooped the last mouthful from his plate and lay back on his swag, his taste buds slathered with pepper and rich smoke. The kangaroo and bush tomatoes had sounded intriguing but tasted better.

He leaned across to Andy. "You should've ordered the kangaroo."

Andy chewed on the last of his chicken and shrugged. The safe option, as Sloaney had jibed before he joined in Lincoln's digs about needing to catch their dessert as it crawled along the crater floor. It was fun while it lasted, until Eliza had shot him a glaring look. He'd taken things too far.

Lincoln studied Andy in the flickering firelight. The go-getter with money behind him seemed to be half the man he used to be, living in a shell that had doubled in size.

Bree's head shaking had started when the plates of kangaroo were handed around. It still shook. "How can you eat something so cute and adorable?"

Lincoln chuckled. "Tell that to the deer we hunt."

Eddie's voice grew louder and he appeared again in the firelight. "All good—she just likes to know where I'm up to with everything." He turned to Eliza as he sat. "You'd love her. Just a wonderful wealth of wisdom lives in that woman."

Eddie stretched with a yawn. "Most tourists can't believe we eat kangaroos, but they're everywhere up here. Tomorrow we'll show you how to find some bush tucker and give you a taste of the real outback." He crossed his legs and laced his fingers behind his head. "There's something about a fire that starts conversations. The fire can draw the truth out of you like it draws the cool from the evening, and your honesty can last as long as the fire is kindled. So why don't you tell me your story?"

Four sets of eyes peeked around the group as if testing the water before jumping in. Lincoln sensed his opportunity in the awkward silence and raised a finger. He held the eye of everyone around the fire to ensure the attention was absolute. He spoke over the crackle of burning wood. "I'll go first. For me, life's very good. Good money and great bonuses. Apartment in Nob Hill and a boat on the Bay."

The flames danced in Eddie's eyes, as his gaze rested on Lincoln. "Do you enjoy it?"

"Loving every minute of life at the moment." Lincoln leaned back onto his swag, as an uncomfortable thought buzzed around him and jostled his pride.

Every minute up until *the letter*.

Andy's voice drifted across the fire. "I'm a bit out of the loop here, but did you go back to Africa?"

Lincoln jammed down the indignation that demanded to burst free. Why should he talk about his life when Andy clearly didn't want anyone prying into his? "No. I moved on to other things." Lincoln forced his gaze onto Andy to stop his glance from drifting to Eliza.

In the crackling silence Eddie gestured to Bree. "So tell me your story."

Bree crept closer to the fire as she pulled the sleeping bag tighter around her. "We're old friends from back in college, and we managed to get through unscathed. Eliza and I kept in touch over the years, but this is the first time we've all been together since."

Sloaney scratched at the earth with a stick. "So what do you do?"

"I've got a part-time job at a recording studio, and when I'm not working, I'm Mom to two and wife to one."

Eddie cocked his head in the half-light. "Do you enjoy it?"

"It's okay. It pays a few bills, and at least I'm still near to music in Nashville. I had a dream to become a musician, but that hasn't really worked out like I hoped."

Eddie shook his head. "That's not what I meant. Do you enjoy being Mum to two and wife to one?"

Bree brightened in the dancing orange light. "Absolutely. I wouldn't swap my family for anything in the world."

Lincoln zoned out of the conversation. What would Eliza reveal when she played her hand? He shuffled the cards he might play next.

"Great to hear about your little ones. Good for you." Eddie's exclamation brought Lincoln back to the crackle of the fire as he gestured to Eliza. "So tell me your story."

Eliza rolled her shoulders and fixed a gaze on Eddie. "I'm in fashion, second-in-charge with a fashion company in Los Angeles called Virgo."

Eddie poked at the coals and a shower of sparks burst

from the ring of stones and flew up into the night. "Do you enjoy it?"

Eliza hesitated, an answer half-escaping from behind tight lips, before she appeared to rein it back in. "Why do you keep asking that?"

"I asked you all to tell me your stories, but so far all you've told me is what you do. That's not your story; that's your job. Your story is where you've come from, which has led to who you are." He raised his hands in defense. "Please don't think I'm having a go—we get so many people out here on a tour, and they all misinterpret the question. They start the trip telling us how important they are, but after a week out here, they're suddenly rethinking what their story is or where they are on the road of life."

Eliza nodded with great enthusiasm. "I appreciate that. I really do. Well, if you want honesty rather than my LinkedIn profile, I've been asked to take over management of my company. I don't want to, and I would like to know why. I feel like my life is lacking something—like I've reached the point where the wood and the trees are virtually indistinguishable. That's the main reason I came."

Lincoln's ears pricked. Now was the moment to insert himself back into this conversation. "I feel you, Lize. Actually when I think about it, work is moving so fast at the moment, it's a lot like a runaway train."

Lincoln's crafted honesty hung in the air unacknowledged

as Eliza continued. "So that's me. I've reached a point in career terms where I'm at the perfect place. People want to be where I am, but I don't. That's why I asked about this walkabout—" She paused with a headshake. "I'm sorry, this journey. It sounded like that sort of discovery would be perfect for me right now."

A silence draped over the crater as Eddie released another shower of sparks into the night air. "You will discover yourself being out here for a while." He swept an arm upward. "Sleeping under the stars. Disconnected from being bothered every five minutes by messages that don't really matter from people you aren't really with. Away from the barrage of overselling of stuff you don't need. Taking a moment to appreciate our world and your place in it."

Andy grunted as he leaned over to grab some wood to throw onto the fire. "Didn't you say on the plane that you wanted to disappear for a while?"

Eliza moved around the campfire closer to Eddie, clearly not willing to let this drop. "So tell me, how do these journeys start?"

"Like all journeys out here. With one step into the desert. For some people, they discover who they really are when it's them alone." Eddie jerked his head toward the darkness. "Out there."

Lincoln's cackle echoed around the crater. "Lize, he's already said we're not doing it."

Her nose crinkled, a sign her heels were sinking into whatever position she couldn't be budged from. "I know, but I want to learn more. I've reached a place in my life where I need to discover who I am. Back in college I was driven and had so much potential and honestly, I was happier. I'm not now."

Bree jumped to her friend's defense. "But you've got the perfect life."

"You keep saying that but, no, I don't. I've got a lot of stuff, but there's something that's missing, and it makes me really unhappy." She sat back from the fire, as if stunned at her own revelation.

Bree's voice dropped to a near whisper. "I didn't know you were so unhappy."

"I didn't realize that until now. I've been trying to work it out for myself rather than burden you."

Bree was close to tears. "But I could have helped."

Watching the exchange, Lincoln felt the buzz within him spread to his extremities. Eliza remembered college as a happier time. And this trip was going to be *significant*. Perhaps a drink might loosen her up. He rummaged through his swag for the vodka he'd bought at the airport.

Another shower of sparks burst into the air from Eddie's stick. "Why don't you let yourself unwind and your nerves untangle and see what happens."

Eliza nodded. "That's probably the best advice I've heard from anyone in the past five years."

Bree scooched farther forward toward the fire. "It's good advice for all of us."

The conversation drifted away on the tendrils of smoke that cut through the chill. Eliza jerked her head toward Andy as dull thuds and the sounds of heavy dragging crept over the crater's lip. Bree tensed as she pointed into the ring of darkness that lurked beyond them. "What was that?"

Sloaney leaned back on his swag and dragged his hat over his face. "Probably roos or a wombat."

Andy stared beyond the light, a strange smile pasted on his face. *What was going on with him?* The outgoing Andy with money was now dodging and weaving and crying poor. Lincoln's annoyance won the battle for control. "Okay, I'll ask. Andy, tell us your story."

Andy jumped as the glassy expression slid from his face, and he appeared to inflate with a sudden joviality. "I like what Eddie says about letting yourself unwind and your nerves untangle."

Lincoln kicked his heel on the stones that circled the fire. "You speak so mysteriously I'm starting to wonder if you work for the CIA."

Andy chuckled, a little too hard. "Not really, but what do I say?"

Eliza spoke into the growing silence. "It was easy for us, Andy. We haven't seen you in five years. What have you been up to?"

Andy's joviality faded. "Working hard, moving around as the work came and went. I'm really enjoying it now in Cincinnati—"

Lincoln sat bolt upright. "At LAX you said were in Chicago."

Eliza braced her hands on her hips. "What's going on? You're evasive, and you avoid your phone like no one else does in the twenty-first century—"

Andy cut her off. "No, you're right, it's Chicago. I moved from Cincinnati not that long ago. I still get those two confused."

Lincoln wasn't buying it. And based on their narrowed eyes and shared glances, neither were Bree or Eliza.

Bree pulled her sleeping bag higher. "It's okay. Even though we haven't seen you for a while, we're still friends—"

"Can I give you some advice, Andy?" Lincoln's impatience got the better of him.

"How about you keep your advice to yourself?" Andy spat out.

Lincoln sat back on his swag, shocked.

The only sound in the crater was the crackle of the dried gum tree consumed by the dancing campfire flames.

———

The coals glowed white hot. The roaring heat of the flames had filtered away with the night, replaced with an intensity from deep within the fire. Eliza wrapped a blanket tighter as the cold air clawed at her shoulders. She lowered her gaze to Andy, his outburst still echoing around the crater. She needed to step in. She had to.

Sloaney closed the lid on the box containing their supplies and sat on it. "How about we talk about what's lined up for tomorrow? We're up early for the outback sunrise, then there's an hour's drive to those hills." He pointed beyond the crater into the dark. "We'll hike into a ravine, try some rock climbing, and might even see some rock carvings. We'll see some wildlife on the way back, then return to camp for some bush tucker, and Eddie will share some of the stories of how this great land came to be."

The thickness of jet lag wrapped around Eliza.

Lincoln stood with a rush. "How about a nightcap before we turn in? I bought something to drink at the airport."

Sloaney threw him a flashlight. "We've got some glasses in the four-wheel drive while you're up there."

Bree wriggled out of her sleeping bag and shivered. "I need something out of my suitcase, so I'll go with you."

They left the circle of light and the flashlight beam swung back and forth in the darkness before it rose out of the crater.

Eliza turned to Andy, whose gaze followed the beam of light. "I need to ask you something. Is it drugs?"

Andy pulled his knees up under his chin. His shaken head gave her the response she hoped for, but his furrowed brow said otherwise. "I haven't touched that stuff since college."

Eliza shifted closer. "Everything about you looks like some people I know back in LA who take drugs. Nervous, evasive, avoiding people or conversations. And if that's you, please tell me and I will try to help if I can."

With a deep breath Andy opened his mouth. Voices grew louder above them, and the flashlight beam swung its way back down the side of the crater. Andy closed his mouth as Eliza leaned forward to fan their sparking connection into a flame. But Andy moved to the woodpile and reached for another log.

Darn it.

Lincoln's indignation stormed back into the campsite before he did. The fire lit up the rippling knots of his clenched jaw. He stomped over to the storage box and placed down six glasses and a large bottle of clear liquid.

Bree shuffled past him and all but collapsed onto her swag. Her makeup case clunked onto the dirt, and confusion washed across her face.

Eliza raised her eyebrows at Bree and mouthed, *What happened?* Bree shook her head.

Lincoln proffered the bottle to Eddie, who again stoked the fire. "Not for me, mate. I'm working."

Eliza raised a hand. "None for me either. I'll stick with water."

The bottle hovered over the glasses and Eliza detected something in Lincoln. A deeper rejection than simply turning down the offer of a drink. Didn't he remember she'd said she didn't touch that stuff anymore?

Eddie stood and stretched. "The first night's always tough, especially with jet lag. If you need something to help you sleep, let me know."

Andy sat up. "What have you got?"

Eliza snapped a look at Bree, then back at Andy. *I knew it.* "Hot chocolate."

Their shared laugher drifted into the air, then silence resumed as they were all drawn into the mesmerizing, pulsing light of the coals. Eliza resolved to revisit that conversation with Andy tomorrow—and make it an intervention if she had to. There was no better place than out here, far away from the influences that had led him down the wrong road.

Andy leaned back on his swag and folded his hands behind his head. "Do you wish you had your guitar, Breezy?"

Sloaney scratched more lines in the dirt. "You play guitar? Are you a good muso?"

Lincoln chimed in. "Back in college she won a chance to record a CD in New York—"

"Wow! New York. You must be great! It's a shame Eddie didn't bring his guitar on this trip."

Bree's eyes glistened in the campfire light, as a twitch tugged on the corner of her lips. Eliza felt compelled to step in, once again the den mother. "New York is the toughest market on earth to crack, but the fact she didn't crack it doesn't make her less of a musician. She gave it her best shot."

Bree winced and stared into the fire, her mouth moving in silence. It was like she was traumatized. Bree should have moved on by now. Unless Lincoln had said something in the darkness fifteen minutes ago . . .

Andy's brow knotted as he reached out a gentle hand. "It's okay if the audition didn't work out."

Lincoln sipped from his glass. "I imagine the audition was hard, Breezy; that's okay. Still, you got to play at the . . . What was the venue?"

Bree eked out in a whisper, "The Apollo Theater."

"What was that like?"

"It was . . ." Bree's sentence trailed off, almost as if she wanted it to drift away on the thin smoke from the campfire. Eliza had to know what was going on. Why couldn't Bree get over this?

"Can't you give me a few details? I was the guy who lent you the money after all."

Bree was silent after Andy's subtle guilt trip dressed up as an innocuous comment. They were all silent.

Lincoln zeroed his spotlight gaze to Andy. "Well, that's it, Andy. You were rolling in money in college. What's happening with you now? We all shared where we are coming from, but we didn't get an answer from you. What's going on?"

Andy stared into the coals.

"Come on, buddy. How about some honesty with your old friends?"

Bree's chest heaved, and her breath became ragged as she shot a look loaded with daggers across the fire at Lincoln. "You're one to talk about honesty."

Her curiosity piqued, Eliza verbally lined up behind her friend. "What is going on?"

Lincoln drained his glass, then stormed out of the circle of light surrounding their campsite, the glow of his phone disappearing into the darkness.

Eliza sighed. She'd come on this trip to find answers to her own questions. But it looked like she'd be called on to fix other people's problems first.

Like she'd always done.

TEN

Lincoln crunched along the rocky track that clung to the cliff wall. He dodged razor-sharp ochre rocks hurled down an age ago. Ahead of him, Eddie's huge backpack disappeared as he bounded down the path like a gazelle, seemingly immune to the constant watch Lincoln needed to keep on his feet.

Bree appeared at his shoulder, as they negotiated a steep section where the path dipped away, sliding down large boulders. The silence was loud.

"Lincoln, I never saw what was in your letter."

Lincoln's chest heaved, and not from the hiking. "I shouldn't have gotten angry with you. It was nothing."

The track took a bend around a sagging gum tree, and Lincoln held back its branches to allow Bree through. Behind them, Eliza was deep in animated conversation with Sloaney. Andy puffed along in their wake. Their vehicle was now a tiny figure at the top of the ridge.

Bree skidded to a halt and turned on him, arms folded. "It seemed more than nothing."

The riverbed rose to meet them as they descended. A wide stretch of sand littered with animal tracks spearing off in every direction. Lincoln had to play it cool, but his self-control failed him. "You were intruding—"

Bree flushed as she angrily waved away a squadron of flies from her face. "But I didn't read anything. What is in it that makes it such a big deal?"

Lincoln measured her for intent and found little evidence of it. "I'm sorry I snapped at you like I did. I guess I'm nervous about talking about a failed marriage, that's all. Can I count on you not to mention it to Eliza? I want to tell her myself."

Bree was quiet for a moment. "If you're serious about rekindling things with her, then you have to tell her. Be honest."

A tiny part of Lincoln flared at that comment, and he had to restrain himself from revisiting old wounds. "Okay, thanks."

Crunching footsteps grew louder and another voice appeared behind them. "Is everything okay?" Eliza.

"Sure." Lincoln angrily charged ahead to catch up to Eddie, who leaned against a stack of fallen rocks, his canteen in hand, as he pointed at the riverbed. "Down there."

Lincoln leaped the final few feet and landed ankle-deep in river sand, throwing a glance over his shoulder. Now Bree and Eliza were deep in discussion. He wanted to believe she would honor her promise, but he couldn't be 100 percent sure.

———

Eliza's shoes sunk into the soft sand of the riverbed as she waved away the flies and tugged on her cap. "So what happened?"

Bree trudged alongside and joined her in what Sloaney kept calling the "Aussie wave." "It all started when we were at the four-wheel drive. Lincoln was having trouble finding that bottle he bought at the airport and an envelope fell out of his suitcase and landed at my feet. I picked it up and handed it back. It's like he changed in a heartbeat, Lize. He blew up and accused me of opening it. I mean, how could I do that? I wouldn't read it anyway."

Harsh screeches descended on them as a flock of white and pink flashed above. The galahs that Sloaney had promised they would see.

"Why would he get so angry?"

"I don't know. I'm hurt that after being honest with him, I get accused of lying."

"I'll confront him."

"No, don't ruin the vacation because of that. It's only a small thing." Bree stopped. "Oh, the crinkle is back. I know what that means."

Eliza huffed as her wave grew more insistent, seemingly attracting more flies than it dispersed. Bree's eyes stayed fixed on the ground. Her lips pursed.

"Was that it?"

Bree seemed to be measuring her words, or restraining them. "Yes. That's all."

"I sense there's more." Eliza looked down at her oldest friend. "Why won't you tell me?"

Bree looked up at her, tears again pricking her eyes. "Why didn't you tell me about how unhappy you were?"

"I'm sorry, Breezy. I told you last night was the first time I've had that thought."

"But you've got everything."

The riverbed widened and Eliza first felt the welcome coolness of water on the air before she saw it. The water hole was a cool oasis in a hot land. A long stretch of deep blue-green water separating pebbles and fine sand from scarred, blood-red rock. Trees dotted the ground, reaching out from under the canopy of the jagged rock wall that rose high above them like a sentinel. Eddie chewed at a gum leaf, his legs swinging from a low limb. Lincoln was nowhere to be seen.

Bree took out her phone. "This is beautiful. Sam would love this and it's definitely Instagram-worthy."

Eliza moved toward Eddie. "Are there many of these gorgeous water holes around the outback?"

"Not really. We had to drive to find this one."

Bree offered her phone to Eddie. "Would you mind?"

"Not at all."

Her arm around Bree, Eliza turned until the background behind them was nothing but slices and scratches on the rock wall. Andy trudged toward them, Sloaney all but carrying him under one arm.

"Where'd the other bloke go?" Eddie handed back the phone.

Eliza shrugged as she sat on the soft sand at the edge of the water hole and unlaced her shoes. She wiped the sweat from her eyes and lowered her toes into the water. The coolness surged through her. Relief. She patted the sand next to her and Bree took a seat.

"Not game enough to put your toes in, Breezy?"

Bree laughed as she hugged her arms to herself. "They'd probably be taken off by a crocodile."

"Out here?"

Birds twittered to their left, the gentle breeze waving through the valley on their right. The soundtrack of the outback bounced back at them from a sounding board carved from ancient rock.

Eliza stretched into the comfortable silence. "I'm so sorry if you felt like I hadn't talked to you last night, but you have to believe me."

"That's okay." Bree smiled. "I'd like to think we're honest with each other."

"Me too." Eliza's forehead puckered and a crinkle appeared above her nose. "Why couldn't you tell us about what it was like to play at the Apollo Theater?"

Bree blanched. "What do you mean?"

"Well, you seemed really upset about that audition, and I would have thought it would be easy to talk about it, that's all."

Bree glared at the sand underneath them, unable—or unwilling—to meet her eyes.

"Come to think of it, I don't think you've ever told me what that audition was like."

Bree's jaw clenched, a quiver on her lip.

"How hard can it be to talk about it? You really need to, even if it's to move on. And I think while we're away would be a good time. When you're ready, I'll be ready to listen."

———

Lincoln's voice rained down on Bree from high up the rock wall. "Get up here. It's amazing!"

Her feet planted firmly in the red sand, Bree held the rope in a limp grip as she squinted up into the fierce blue of the afternoon sky. Her two helmeted friends dangled above her, swinging against the jagged wall. There was no chance of her joining them. Not with her fear of heights.

The third rope remained empty and still. While Andy

had reluctantly scaled to the top, he hadn't reappeared. Perhaps Eddie was talking him down.

Bree took out her phone. In every direction was a picture-perfect scene waiting for capture. The girls would have loved this. Sam too. She sighed hard. They would never travel as a family without some kind of financial miracle. Her dream of seeing the world had withered with her dream of a musical career. She stepped closer to a bush, its thin, olive-green leaves studded with bursts of white and yellow flowers. She held up her phone for another postcard image.

"It's wattle, and it's edible."

Bree jumped a mile as Sloaney appeared behind her. "The flowers?"

"No, the seeds. Grind them into flour and make bread. The bush is full of life, you know."

"What else can you eat from this bush?"

Sloaney beamed. "Not *this* bush, *the* bush." He strode to a squat bush laden with rich-red berries. He snapped off a few and popped them in his mouth, biting down hard, the juice dribbling down his chin. The other berries balanced on his weathered hand. "Here."

Bree took one and gingerly placed it between her lips. She bit down, and a tart burst of sweet juice flooded her mouth.

Sloaney grinned as he shoved the remaining berries into his mouth. "See? Full of life." He marched to the base of the cliff and steadied one of the ropes gyrating wildly. "Lincoln! Legs straight like I told you."

The rope slowed its frenetic swinging and Sloaney rejoined her. "There is life out here—food everywhere, clean air, clean water. I wouldn't live anywhere else for a million bucks."

"How does it all stay alive when it doesn't rain?"

Sloaney chuckled as he pointed beyond the wall on which her friends dangled. "I'll take care of your mates. Follow the path. You'll find some rock carvings that have been there for millennia. Go ahead and have a look, but no photos please. The rock carvings are sacred and we respect that."

Bree walked past the dangling ropes and followed a track that veered around the cliff's base. Twenty yards later, the path was split in two by an enormous gum tree, its mottled branches jutting beyond the shade into sunlight. Underneath it sat a rounded boulder, long sweeping scratches adorning its surface. She padded along the track, and as she stood in front of it, she only saw thick gouges in the rock that occasionally crossed, smaller sweeps that lost their meaning.

It was no longer a picture. She felt, rather than saw, the slightest movement a couple of feet above her head. Her heart started to pound as she let her eyes drift slowly up, and she gazed into the softest, fluffiest, most gorgeous face of the one creature she wanted to see on this trip.

In the crook of the mottled branches sat a koala, nonchalantly chewing eucalyptus leaves while surveying her with casual disdain.

"Oh, how beautiful." Bree raised her phone and rattled off nearly a hundred photos.

"You're gorgeous." She eased her hand toward it. The chewing slowed and the koala's eyes narrowed.

"I wouldn't do that if I were you." Sloaney moved in next to her. "Take all the photos you want, but I'd leave that fella alone."

"Why is that? He's adorable."

"See how he's holding on to the gum tree? You wouldn't want to get in the way of those, and there's the chlamydia too."

Long, thick nails like talons sprung from the ends of the koala's claws and were embedded in the tree.

"Wild koalas aren't as cute as you think they might be, but I think your girls might like a photo of you two together."

Bree handed over her phone and backed slowly, nervously, toward the tree, one eye fixed on the koala, whose interest in Bree had all but evaporated.

"Smile, you'll be fine." Sloaney took a picture, then handed back her phone. "Fantastic!"

Bree snuck one last look at the koala. "Now all I need to see is a kangaroo."

"We'll be lucky to see one during the day. Wait until dusk and you'll see mobs of them. Now, these rock carvings. Come with me." He curled his finger and Bree followed him back along the path. He turned her shoulders until she was facing the carved boulder again.

"Now you're standing in the best place to see it. Everyone goes too close and they lose the perspective."

The lines converged, their sweeping breadth joining together to make sense. Bree could make out a turtle or some kind of animal. A harsh, rich cackle burst from the trees on the ridge above their path and Bree ducked.

Sloaney reached for the near-vertical rock wall. "That's a kookaburra. A beautiful bird. There's no need to worry about him." He scaled the first few feet. "I've got to get up there and rescue your friend. Lincoln is giving him a hard time." Bree's gaze followed Sloaney as he clambered up the wall.

Eliza rounded the corner as she unclipped her helmet. "What have you found?"

She pointed to the rock carvings. "You can look, but you have to be here to get the right perspective."

"Perspective, a good lesson."

"But that's not all. Follow me. Quietly."

They padded along the path to the gum tree and its lone occupant. "Oh, how gorgeous. How soft is his fur?" Eliza reached out a hand but Bree stopped her. "Sloaney said not to touch him, check out his claws, and you can get chlamydia."

Eliza shot a quick glance at Bree, lowered her hand but raised her phone. They rattled off a dozen photos—together and alone with the koala. She peered past Bree at the corner of the path. "Can I talk to you?"

She really didn't want to talk about the audition. Not now.

"It's Andy. We need to help him. Will you support me if we have an intervention?"

"Of course." Relief flooded through Bree. The time to talk about the audition wasn't now—she needed time to prepare for the inevitable. Eliza's unhappiness that Bree had kept such a big secret for fifteen years from her best friend from college.

ELEVEN

Andy burned with embarrassment. Sloaney had lowered him from the cliff top like a removalist shifting a piano from a penthouse. Andy needed some time on his own, time to think. Time to fume. He sat on the flat rock, his feet dangling in the water as he looked deep into the water hole. The bottom was down there somewhere, below the murky blue-green. The water could have been feet deep or miles.

Andy had always been able to wave away criticism, but Lincoln's antagonism had slipped under his skin. Had he known that Lincoln had changed like this, Andy probably wouldn't have come.

He shook his head with a bitter laugh. Who was he kidding? That wasn't true. This was the price to pay—hopefully the last price he would pay for a while.

The bushes behind him rustled. Silence. The leaves shook again, and Andy glanced around for a rock. Anything. The leaves parted as a face pushed through the scrub. Two beady eyes focused on him. A twitch of the ears. An inquisitive cock of the sloping, pointed head.

A kangaroo.

Andy sat dead still, his heart pounding, unwilling to surprise the animal two feet from him. Didn't they kick with powerful legs when they felt threatened?

Strings of grass worked their way around the kangaroo's mouth—like a cow working its cud. It placed gentle hands on the ground as if to steady itself and hopped its back legs closer to the water hole and him. Andy was within touching distance of an Australian icon. It slowly worked the grass, the sun catching the sheen of its gray-and-brown coat. Ears twitching 180 degrees. He reached out a slow hand to pat it and the chewing stopped.

Sweat funneled down Andy's temples, drawing the flies. He fought hard against the urge to wave away their itching annoyance. "It's okay."

The kangaroo bounded backward into the bush in one hop at the sound of Andy's voice and was gone.

Andy ducked for cover, his pulse again pounding in his ears as the adrenaline coursed through him. Lincoln appeared at the cliff top, backing up to the edge. The indignation flushed out the adrenaline.

"Come on, Andy, get up here!"

Andy fumed. Lincoln had played some stupid competitive

macho game in front of Eliza and accused him of slowing them down. Andy's place in the world—to use Eddie's words—had started with Lincoln's words. One piece of information that had won a short-term victory but triggered a series of long-term losses. A resentment toward his old friend rose, but now Eliza was also on his case, and once she got hold of something, she didn't let go.

Andy exhaled hard as he kicked his legs in the cool water and waved away another advancing wave of flies. He didn't want to talk about why he wanted to disappear. He needed a clean break, where no one knew his name or his history.

Behind him the bushes rustled again. Andy made a slow turn, his lesson learned, but the bushes rustled higher than they did before. Higher than they should for a kangaroo.

In front of him, bubbles blooped to the water's surface near his feet, and Andy felt a brushing against his toes.

"Ahhh!" He scrambled to his feet.

"Ahhh!" Eliza jumped back into greenery from which she'd emerged. "What are you doing? You scared the life out of me."

Andy shook the water from his toes as he counted them. "There's something down there, and it nearly had me for lunch."

Eliza placed a caring hand on Andy's arm and smiled. "You wandered off. Are you okay?"

He stepped back from her probing concern. "I'm a little shaken after a kangaroo scares the life out of me and a monster from the deep tries to drag me in."

Eliza sat on the large, flat rock and patted the space next to her. Andy set his feet and folded his arms.

"I came to ask if you'd like to continue the conversation we had last night. You never got a chance to answer my question about whether or not you needed help."

Andy stared at the rock wall and the deep water, his mind ticking it over. In a way, owning up to drugs might be easier. "All I want to do is enjoy this trip, okay?"

The crinkle above Eliza's nose deepened. "If something is holding you back . . . Something from the past?"

Lincoln appeared at the top of the wall for the third time, helmeted and attached to the rope. "Woohoo!" He waved at Eliza and his taunting chant rained down. "Two-nil. Two-nil. Two-nil. Two-nil."

Andy bit his lip hard until he could taste the salt of his own blood. He wanted this conversation to end, and for this part of his life to end, without being given the third degree. He tingled with hurts long buried but recently uncovered; nerves exposed to the air. "You want to have a conversation about our pasts? How about you talk to Lincoln about how he started all this for me back in college?"

Eliza powered between the fallen rocks, as she forged up the path that led from the gorge, shuffling the pieces of conversation she'd been drawn into. That she needed to fix.

Crunching steps grew closer. The stride was too long for Bree, too purposeful for Andy.

She turned and Lincoln's sweaty, smiling face filled her vision. She stepped aside to let him pass, but he instead ushered her to lead the way and he fell in behind her. "Can we talk?"

"Sure. I was hoping to get a moment to chat with you as well."

Eliza waved away the flies and brushed off the sweat pooling under the peak of her cap. They ascended in silence, Eliza waiting for whatever Lincoln wanted to say.

"I guess you officially win the competition for most successful."

She turned on her heel and stopped on the path. Lincoln skidded to a halt, his nose inches from hers. "Really, Lincoln? Is that what this is about? I've reached a point in my life where I'm wondering about the value of all that, so I'm not really interested in competitions or success. Goodness knows I'm not impressed by it, if you haven't worked that out."

He took a sheepish backward step as she took the wind out of his sails.

She sighed. "I'm sorry, I don't want there to be bad blood

spoiling the vacation." She waved a hand around them. "Not out here in paradise."

Lincoln nodded. "You're right. Let's keep going."

Eliza resumed the climb. He kept bringing up his success—at first bragging about it, now downplaying it. What was his game?

"Do you mind if I ask you one question?" Lincoln's words now came between puffs of exertion.

"Sure." Eliza braced herself.

"What did you mean by being lost in life?"

Eliza relaxed, warmed by his interest. "I think I've been chasing this dream, and now I'm wondering if it was the right dream in the first place."

"But Bree said you have the perfect life—career, apartment, car, party scene." A pause grew, pregnant with intent. "Lots of guys."

Eliza tensed. She knew when a conversation was being led somewhere. "Maybe life is more than that."

"So you don't have anyone in your life at the moment?" Lincoln's question trailed up with a lightness that felt forced.

Her suspicion ran ahead of her, waving frantic flags. Eliza slowed her pace and closed her eyes, reining in control of her breathing to center herself. Her pulse slowed as the moment arrived. "Do you?"

"Not anyone serious. At the moment."

Eliza could feel Lincoln tense behind her as he fell silent. This was not the old Lincoln who could have represented his country if talking were an Olympic sport. "Can I ask you something?"

"Sure. Anything."

"What was so bad about a letter that made you snap at Bree?"

"It was a misunderstanding."

"But she's really upset, and whatever's in there, she didn't read it."

"Fine. I'll apologize again."

"And you didn't answer my question." She turned to him, and his gaze drifted to her nose. "Tell me if I'm prying."

"You're prying."

The screeches of the white-and-pink galahs filled her ears as Eliza resumed the climb. One minute Lincoln was concerned about her, the next he was quizzing her about her private life while slamming doors on his own. The old dynamic threatened to scratch its way to the surface, and she didn't want to let it back out. Not fifteen years later.

Eliza stepped onto a finger of rock that stretched over the riverbed a hundred feet below. The metal security fence creaked, sagging as she leaned on it, and Lincoln joined her. The wind whipped at the wisps of hair escaping from under her cap as she pulled out her canteen. "We need to talk about Andy. I'm really concerned about him. I'm wondering if he's got a drug problem, so can we talk to him tonight around the fire? As friends?"

Lincoln's eyes softened, the eyes Eliza had lost herself in ages ago. She batted away the sparking reconnection. "Of course. That makes sense. He's been pretty cagey since we all met in LA."

Above them, a wedge-tailed eagle screeched to a midflight halt, a hovering fixture in a crystal-blue sky unblemished by clouds.

Back down the path, Bree's and Eddie's heads appeared on their way up.

"Andy said one other thing down there at the water hole. He said you started all his problems back in college."

Lincoln shrugged, his face a blank slate. "No idea. Started off his problems? With what?"

The distant chatter drifted up to the lookout. Lincoln's leg muscles rippled in the sun, and Eliza forced herself to stay in the present.

Lincoln leaned against her. "You know it's good to talk again, Lize. It's been ages since we've been able to talk properly. We could talk about anything back in school."

Eliza shook her head. Lincoln had been more than an old friend in college until she'd drawn the curtain across it—and she hadn't spoken to him "properly" in more than a decade.

Lincoln stared into the reflective blue-green of the water hole below, the wind tousling his brown hair. Like it used to.

"You know, I've always wondered what our lives would have been like had we stayed together."

And there it was. She had to put a stop to it. Now.

Eliza turned to him and folded her arms with a hint of defense. "We were kids back then, and we didn't know what we wanted."

Lincoln's eyes were no longer hard but soft. College soft. "To be perfectly honest with you, I haven't had a relationship that's worked out since."

Eliza's resolve steeled. She didn't want to rehash things that belonged in the past, much less be blamed for them. As much as she had told Bree before their flight that she'd moved on, it was becoming clear that Lincoln hadn't. And he was using her as the reason to stay stuck in the past.

━━━━━

Andy leaned against the four-wheel drive as the group disappeared into the scrub to take in yet another wonder of nature. He had to fast-track his plans, and Eliza would not be the ally he had hoped for. She was fast becoming the biggest threat.

Sloaney rounded the vehicle. "You coming with us, mate?"

Andy nodded. "In a minute."

"What are you thinking about?"

"Taking some time off and working out here, maybe at a cattle station."

Sloaney bobbed his head. "I've got a mate who's got a place. A small holding, only about a quarter of a million acres."

Perfect. "Could you put me in touch with him?"

"Sure. What can you offer?"

That was a question Andy had never considered. A job in the outback wasn't something to do. It was somewhere to go.

Sloaney leaned in with a whisper. "What's your deal?"

Andy stood back as he tried to pump genuine indignation into his voice to conceal his anxiety. "Deal? No deal. I thought working in Australia for a while might be fun."

Sloane's eyes narrowed. "I could put you in touch, but there aren't a lot of jobs out here at the moment, with the drought and everything. Maybe when we get back into town?"

"I'd like to call them before that if I could. Maybe on your satellite phone?"

Sloaney folded his arms. "Why all the cloak-and-dagger stuff? Aren't you all flying back through Sydney to the States?"

Andy's breath caught in his throat, and he nearly choked as the flies found his gaping mouth. He spluttered as he regained his composure.

Sloaney hadn't moved, one eyebrow now cocked. "You sound like you're not planning on going home at all."

TWELVE

Bree breathed through her sleeve as choking plumes of red bone-dry dirt flung into the air. Eddie's spade bit into the ground below a wholly unremarkable olive-leaved bush.

"So if we go down here . . ."

Bree blanched at the thought of what he was searching for. She stood back, less for her own safety from this flashing blade and more to put distance between her and these "grubs." She wasn't eating bugs—chicken-tasting or not. Not when there was real chicken back at the campsite. She had hit her limit with the red berries Eddie had found. They were sweet and tart. There. She could say she'd eaten bush food.

Thunk. Eddie's spade hit something solid. "Perfect. Here we go." He reached for a tomahawk and chopped at the thick ropey roots. The ax's blade flashed in the sun as his sinewy brown forearms strained under sweat.

Eddie sighed as he removed a foot-long tree root and held it up. "He's in there."

Lincoln took it from Eddie and peered into the end. "I'm not sure what I'm looking for."

Eddie peeled away the root's skin with practiced fingers. The slow wriggle of the witchetty grub held Bree spellbound. Eddie squeezed gently and pulled it out. Two inches of thick, white larva squirming in the sun. "Who'd like a taste?"

Lincoln hesitated for a moment, then Eliza elbowed him out of the way. She winced as she chewed. "It's kind of . . . I don't know." She smiled. "It's pleasant. Like cooked eggs."

Lincoln snatched the remainder of the grub from her and shoved it into his mouth. "It's soft . . . almost buttery." He swallowed with a loud gulp. "Can you find another one for Bree?"

Bree backed away as Eliza said, "You've got to take a chance once in your life."

Eddie stood and wiped dusty hands on his shorts. "So there's the witchetty grub you wanted me to find, but now I want to show you there's more to bush food than that." He pushed through the foliage that swept over the thin, unobtrusive path.

Eliza raced up to him, leaving Bree alone on the path. "What are we looking for?"

Eddie peered into the bush. "Quandongs. They're a type

of native peach. Bush bananas too. Some native plums if we can find them. It's like a dessert bar out here."

Bree watched the foliage swallow her group and she was left alone. She couldn't do it. She'd end up doubled over vomiting or poisoned. Or worse. She wasn't up to taking chances. And no amount of dressing up weird food as a "dessert bar" was going to help.

A light breeze whisked away the voices of the group, and she stood alone in the middle of a continent. Silence, punctuated by a harsh twittering from above and rustling from the ground on either side of the path; sounds cloaked by tall grass and low trees. Brown and olive green floating on a sea of red. She felt a sense of wonder at the landscape's beauty, and a sense of her own insignificance in its shadow.

She took two steps in the direction the voices had gone. The path was now blocked.

"Eddie?" Her thin voice elongated two curt syllables into three long ones.

In the middle of the path a long, black snake coiled back on itself. It appeared to be gathering energy to strike. At her.

Bree flushed cold in the heat as she froze. "Eddie?" Three more long syllables.

The snake eyed her from the path, the sun rippling from its dark-brown scales. Its head eased back into its body.

The foliage parted. "Don't. Move." Eddie stepped off the path and inched around the snake, his eyes not deviating from the threat. The snake sensed his movement and jerked back.

Eddie stepped in front of Bree and placed an arm across her, his voice flat. "I want you to take a step back. Slowly. He doesn't like sudden movements."

Bree's heart pounded as she fought to rein in the numbing panic. Behind the added protection of Eddie's arm, she backed away, then collapsed against a gum tree.

The foliage parted again, and Lincoln stormed onto the path.

Eddie raised his arms, his voice like flint. "Stay there."

Lincoln dropped his gaze to the snake and inched back as he proffered the shovel. "Here, you'll need this."

Eddie waved him away. "Stay where you are. Dangerous fella, this one, and we're going to let him go on his way."

Lincoln took a step forward as he gripped the shovel tight. "Why wouldn't you kill him?"

"Once we've gone and moved on with our lives, we'll leave him to move on with his."

Bree watched the snake as it watched Eddie and Eddie watched it. Despite its deadly danger, this reptile conveyed a quiet majesty, a slow purpose to its movements. Bree's breath returned as the snake uncoiled, relaxing, its head shifting left and right, eyeing an exit.

Eddie put up his hands and took a slow step toward it. "Careful now. Careful." His toes tapped slowly on the path, mesmerizing the snake as it continued to uncoil. "Careful now. Careful."

The snake slithered off the path and slunk into the bush, taking an age for its body to disappear into the scrub.

Eddie padded forward and inspected its exit point before he gestured to them. "He's gone. We can go now."

Bree's heart resumed its frantic rhythm as they crept past, her eyes fixed on the low grass, sure the snake was waiting for the others to pass before it lunged at her. But the grass was still.

Once she was clear, her jog graduated into a sprint, and her heart still pounded as she rushed into Eliza's arms, the sobs coming as the terror leaked away.

———

Lincoln slammed the car door as the late-afternoon shadows painted the landscape a pastel purple and yellow. The ride back to the campsite had been cloaked in an unhappy quiet despite Sloaney's attempts to start conversation. Lincoln charged toward the crater's lip, the setting sun blocked by the top of the dirt skyscraper. He leaned on it, his shoulders hunched, his head down, his breathing racing away from him. Things were unraveling. Fast.

Andy huffed and wheezed his way past him.

"What do you mean I'm to blame for your problems?"

Andy grimaced as he hefted his backpack higher on his shoulder. "What do you mean?"

"Eliza told me I was to blame for your problems." Huffing, he puffed back his shoulders. "If you've got something to say, say it. And if you don't, you should probably take responsibility for your own life." He turned on his heel and leaped into the crater, the soft sand cradling his descent. He felt better—at least he'd addressed that issue. That left one—his reason for coming—and his chances with Eliza were slipping away.

THIRTEEN

The turquoise of the sky was brushed by reds and oranges as it submitted to the inky blackness of the night.

Silence, spoiled only by the crackle of the deadwood as it gave itself to the fire. Silence, fueled by unspoken tension that had risen like floodwaters throughout the day.

Raindrops speckled Eliza's hand as more fizzled on the fire, the hint of water growing on the breeze. The maelstrom of strange tastes and sensations swirled around her mouth— the dense heaviness of the damper bread, the strange sweetness of goanna, and the tart tang of native plums, flavored by an earthy spice from her plate of paperbark.

Eddie gently blew on a smoldering branch. The edges of its leaves glowed red in the half-light. "I was going to share some of my stories, but it might be better to clear the air, if you don't mind me saying, and around the fire is the perfect place." He leaned away into the darkness as Eliza leaned in.

"Thanks, Eddie." His words were perfect, exactly what he had promised. She drew from the thoughts she had pieced together as the outback scrolled past her window on the drive back from the gorge. She would deal with Lincoln later. Andy had to be first.

She turned to him as he stared blankly into the fire from inside the cowl of his hoodie. "Andy. We really do care about you and want to do something. We're all friends and we're here for you."

Bree nodded enthusiastically. Lincoln's brows furrowed in a concerned nod. Eliza was glad he'd been able to put aside his angst for their old friend.

Andy pulled his hoodie tighter, his gaze darting anywhere but at Eliza. "What are you doing?"

"You reached out last night around the fire, but circumstances prevented us from finishing that conversation, and it's an important one. We are ready to listen, and if we can help you, we will."

Andy exhaled hard as he stared at the stars.

"I've helped a number of friends when they've had issues with drugs. I can help you too." Eliza leaned back on her swag, pleased she'd delivered her message as she planned.

Bree reached out to Andy. "It's okay."

The trickle of a giggle leaked from inside Andy's cowl, before his bulk quivered with a hearty, bitter laugh.

Bree's brows knotted in confusion and Lincoln shrugged.

Andy threw a narrow-eyed glare at Eliza. "I've already told you I haven't touched drugs since college."

Eliza started an unexpected backpedal, and Lincoln raised a finger as he stepped in. "You've been evasive since we met in LA. You've avoided all conversations about your life, and you're apparently snippy at me because I somehow did something in college. What the heck is going on?"

Andy's laugh stopped dead as he now aimed his glare at Lincoln. "Thanks, Mr. Successful, dripping in money, giving advice to all and sundry. Well, your advice *isn't* always the greatest."

A large branch leaning across the fire collapsed into the flames, puffing up a gray cloud of ash that wafted away in the growing breeze. A flash of lightning illuminated the darkening turquoise of the sky.

Lincoln broke a stick in two before he threw it onto the fire. "What are you talking about? I told you an hour ago you need to take responsibility for your life—"

Eliza inched toward Andy. "So if it's not drugs, what is it?"

Andy pulled the cowl farther forward. Hunks of steaming, rhythmic breath escaped his cowl.

This was working. He had to acknowledge he needed help. The first step was always the hardest—acknowledging you couldn't do this on your own.

Bree's smile seemed forced. "It might be better if you talk about your life."

The puffs of steam grew more insistent as Andy's shoulders heaved. "You want to know why I don't feel like talking about my life? It's because I want to run away from it, that's why."

Eliza sighed with a subdued smile. A breakthrough, albeit a sad one. While she was able to ignore Lincoln's insecure competition about success, Andy wasn't. It was hurting him, and he needed to know it wasn't a game worth playing. "It's not about keeping up with others or even how much you earn, it's—"

Andy's caustic laugh forced her to jump. "You can never earn enough when you've got a massive gambling problem."

"Gambling? I thought it was far worse than that."

Andy buried his head in his hands. "It *is* far worse."

The coals sizzled again as another drift of raindrops found the fire. Eliza mouthed to Lincoln, *Say something*. Lincoln simply shrugged. Eliza inched closer to Andy. "What can we do?"

Andy's head shot up. "How about you go back in time and tell my college self to ignore Captain Moneybags here." He jerked his head at Lincoln before rounding on him. "You know what was so bad about that tip you gave me back in college? It wasn't that I lost money; it was that I won, and I won big. I lived it up and went back to that well when that money ran out and then I lost it all, but it sparked something that's controlled me ever since."

Andy's bulk heaved, his breath short and sharp as he looked across the fire to Eddie. "You talked about journeys? At this point in my"—his fingers provided the sarcastic air quotes—"journey, if I could start again with a clean slate and no debts, I would be fine. I would never gamble again."

Lincoln frowned. "But you always had money in college. You threw the biggest graduation party—"

"Yeah, I did—all from that one tip from you on the massive underdog in Flagstaff College going up against the might of number-one seed Clarendon University—and I wanted to share the love. I even lent money for Bree to go to that audition in New York, and I never saw that again."

Bree's mouth dropped open. Eliza threw an arm around her shoulders—even in the orange light she was pale. "Don't bring her into your problems."

The gusting wind flicked at the ropes of their swags and a distant rumble rolled over the lip of the crater and washed over them.

Eliza squeezed Bree's shoulder. This hadn't gone at all like she'd planned, but at least there was one upside to Andy's rant—maybe this was the chance for Bree to deal with her baggage once and for all. "It's okay to let it out. So you auditioned and it didn't work out. You need to come to terms with your disappointment and move on. At least you were brave enough to try."

Bree dissolved in a flood of sobbing and mumbling into

Eliza's chest. Three small words Eliza didn't quite catch. "What was that?"

Bree's voice drifted up to Eliza among snatches of wind and spitting coals. "I wasn't brave."

Eliza held silent, allowing the space for her friend's story to finally come out into the open where it could be addressed. "You were brave, Breezy. You took your chance in the big city, stood proudly in the spotlight, and gave it your best. You put yourself out there when you walked onto that stage."

Bree trembled under her arm. Another three small words, but this time Eliza caught them. They didn't make any sense. "What did you say?"

Bree sat up, her cheeks glistening with tears, her cracking voice thin. Wavering. "I never went."

"What do you mean you never went?"

"I got as far as the foyer, but I turned around and walked out."

Lincoln's mouth dropped open. Eliza could feel the heat pulsing not from the fire but from her left. Andy.

Eliza blinked hard. She had carried her friend through the bitter disappointment of a failed audition. "You lied to me?"

Bree's sobs wracked her with tremors, punctuating any words that found their way out in sputtering fits and starts. "Wouldn't get it . . . couldn't do it . . . letting everyone down . . . I'm so sorry."

Eliza forced her thoughts into order. "When I asked you

why they turned you down, you told me they were looking for someone with more soul. That was a lie?"

"So . . . sorry . . . Lize." Bree buried her head deeper into Eliza's chest.

Andy kicked at the stones around the fire. "You're joking? I gave you money to fulfill your dream—money I needed to deal with my own demons—and you blew it on a free trip to New York?"

Lincoln rose to his full height, hands on hips, and moved to stand next to Bree. "You can't throw that back on her. You dug your own hole."

Andy's eyes narrowed as he stood. "You're one to talk—you told me I couldn't lose but you were wrong. When I lost, I lost big."

"Yeah? How big?"

The heart of the fire released another shower of sparks to the gusting wind. Sloaney rushed to brush the embers from the swags, now dotted in glowing ashes.

Andy looked into the night. "As of right now? Seven hundred thousand dollars." He arrowed a sarcastic glance at Eliza. "See? Far worse."

Lincoln's finger quivered at Andy. "You can't blame everyone else for that. It's like when I'm working with my clients. I give them stockbroking advice and they decide if they want to follow it."

Andy sneered. "Really? Do you give them that speech

when your advice is bad for them, and they lose all their money? It's not your fault?"

Eliza's mind whirled as it scrambled for a grip on anything tangible. Her planned intervention was more than a failure. It was severing old ties. How did they get here so quickly? She had to get them back on track. "What can we do for you, Andy?"

He pulled his hoodie tight around him, shoulders hunched. A beaten man—one who had taken on the world but cowered on the canvas with rounds still to fight. "How about you leave me alone? Leave me to do what I wanted to do. Disappear."

Eliza kept her voice flat. Unthreatening. "You can't do that."

He turned on his heel. "Watch me." Andy stormed between the swags and beyond the safe circle of light around the campfire. With the crunch of gravel and the soft thud of feet climbing the crater wall, he was gone.

Eliza reached out to her two remaining old friends. "We should go after him."

Lincoln leaned away from the fire. "Leave him. We're not responsible for him or his problems."

Eddie's gaze followed Andy into the darkness as the sky flashed turquoise again. "I'll go after him in a few moments."

Silence, spoiled only by the spitting of rain on glowing coals and the gentle flap of canvas crinkling in the breeze. Silence, amplified as the unspoken tension ratcheted up another notch in between shallow breaths and the choking back of tears.

Lincoln stared at Andy's empty swag as Sloaney watched him from across the campfire. "Are you okay, mate?"

Lincoln nodded as Eliza rushed to wrap a blanket around Bree. He processed the last ten minutes, but the temerity of Andy's accusation jagged on his self-righteousness. He was tired of people blaming him for their unhappiness. "This isn't our fault. He's got to own up to what's going on in his life and be honest with himself."

Bree's voice emerged from under the blanket. "That's rich coming from you."

Lincoln felt like he'd been slapped. "Why is this about me?"

Bree threw off the blanket and glared at him. "You like having things in the open, do you? If you want Andy to be honest, how about you start? You hide a huge thing from us about being married—so much for your honesty."

Eliza nearly snapped her neck as she spun to face Lincoln. "You what?"

Oh no. Lincoln's pulse quickened. "Since when do I have to report to everyone about what's going on in my life?"

Eliza wasn't backing down. "You're married?"

This was not how he wanted Eliza to find out. "It was a mistake."

"And you didn't think your old friends would be interested in knowing that?" Eliza's head shake grew in intensity. "And you talk to me about rekindling things?"

Bree shuffled around the fire to join Eliza as the breeze gusted into a steady wind. "What's in that letter that so terrifies you if we know about it?"

The battle inside Lincoln raged as the rejection from his youth and the rejection of the present melded to form an unstoppable force. The mercury inside him rose as the wind rushed through the campsite, extinguishing the remaining flame clinging to life on unburned wood. "You want to know what's in the letter? My very-soon-to-be ex-wife wants a divorce, and she's coming after the fortune I amassed from my sheer talent and fifteen years of working hard. And she's coming after me for more than her fair share. She wants it all."

Eliza thrust out her hands. "Well, tell her she can't have it. Why would she do something like that?"

Lincoln folded his arms as the story he wanted to stay closed was pried open inch-by-inch. "She kept going on about all these other women—"

Eliza scoffed. "I can see why. Your social media over the last year or so has been nothing but you and other women."

Lincoln raised a deliberate, quivering finger and pointed it at her. "Don't you lecture me on relationships. None of that happened before she left. Look, it's no big deal."

It was as if Bree's voice was strengthened by being next

to Eliza. "No big deal? You got married! Why wouldn't you tell us?"

The wind now howled through the campsite, embers sailing as Eddie rushed to check the swags. "We weren't expecting any kind of weather tonight."

Lincoln wasn't expecting anything like this either. He struggled to hear Eliza's voice over the wind. "Wait a minute! You are *still* married?"

Lincoln shielded his eyes from the sand that swirled throughout the crater. "She kicked me to the curb."

"But you were still married and that would have crushed her. It would probably feel like you'd already moved on and left her behind."

The fuse that had been slow burning for fifteen years flared to life with Eliza's comment. "And there it is. You did exactly the same thing to me at graduation—moved on with your life without even looking back or asking me if this was a direction we could go in together. Who packs their bags for LA and moves on without looking back?"

"Lincoln, I was trying to—"

"What? Do what was best for you? And then you built this perfect life that revolves around you."

The wind flung Bree's blanket high into the air, where it disappeared into the darkness. "How different is that from your life? You never were like this, Lincoln, but now you're all about yourself."

He wasn't finished with Eliza. "You said this trip was going to be significant. What does that even mean?"

"It means something is missing in my life, and I'm taking the time to find out what it is."

Eddie returned to the campfire. "We should think about finding Andy—"

"Shush!" Bree raised a hand. "Can you hear that?"

Beyond the gusts of wind, there was a different sound. A heaviness. A rushing. Like a distant freight train.

Eddie threw a panicked look at Sloaney. "That sounds like it's going to hit us."

Bree stood. "It sounds like a train."

Eddie shook his head. "No trains around here."

The roar grew louder, deeper, and in an instant the campsite was lashed with a gale-force wind, knocking them off their feet.

Bree yelled, "It's a hurricane. We have to find Andy."

Sloaney cupped his hands around his mouth. "We don't get hurricanes out here. Get to the four-wheel drive. Hopefully Andy's got enough sense to find it."

Eddie yelled into the howling wind, "I'll go and find him." A faint flashlight beam rushed away from the camp as the dust circled the crater, the campfire seemingly in the eye of the storm.

Eliza stood, hands on her hips. "That was fifteen years ago and I've moved on."

Sloaney grabbed Lincoln's arm. "We have to get to the vehicle."

Lincoln shook him off as fifteen years of unresolved grief demanded their moment. He cupped his hands, his voice hoarse from the dust. "And yet here you are, claiming you're lost in the world and something is missing. I reckon the missing piece of your puzzle is me."

"Were you hoping to invite me to the other side of the world and just pick up where we left off? Do you really think I'm that same woman who had just graduated from college?"

Lincoln had to make his point. He couldn't lose this exchange. "Isn't that what you wish you were anyway? Back when you were happy?"

A rock the size of Lincoln's fist flew past his nose, and Sloaney groaned as he doubled over. "There's no time. Stay low and get into the swags."

Above the crater and the screaming wind, a car door slammed. Lincoln dived into his swag, the canvas crumpling in the wind. Dust hit the swag like a sandblaster, and with fumbling fingers he zipped it up. The stinging stopped but the roaring continued. Lincoln lay in the deafening noise, his mind racing, his pulse thudding in his ears. When this storm had passed, a long list of people would get a piece of his mind.

And at the front of that line was Eliza.

FOURTEEN

Andy tried to squint away the pain behind his eyes as he rubbed his temples. Last night was a blur—the attack from the others, scrambling to find the four-wheel drive for shelter, walking against an impossible wind and its scalding, sandblasting dust. Stumbling across the swags.

The wind whipped at a rope scratching at his swag as the confines of his tiny sleeping quarters warmed with the early morning sun—the tucked-away solitude of his own space, the others zipped up on the outside. He reached for his cell phone. Seven a.m., and the solitude extended to his place in the world. No coverage.

Relief. Andy strained to hear if anyone else was up. The expected muttering and whispered gossip, continuing their intervention but this time focused on another vice. His secret was now out but so was his escape plan. He was sure it would be the first topic of conversation over breakfast.

Something sailed on the breeze, a faint smell that was both familiar and yet hard to pinpoint. It wasn't the burning eucalyptus from last night. That smell was etched into his memory—smoke, menthol, and something elusive. No, this smell was fresh, like the eucalyptus at the water hole. Eddie must have brought in some branches. Maybe Eliza was getting her wish to do a . . . What did she call it? Journey of discovery?

Andy shook his head with a sigh. It sounded like one of those motivational seminars back home, but the corporate arena had been replaced by the middle of nowhere and the shaman had traded slicked-back hair and a pin-striped suit for the exotic mystique of an ancient culture.

A throaty chuckle burst from above his swag, graduating into a harsh cackling laugh. It wasn't human. Andy clicked open the zip to see a bird perched on a gum tree's limb above him, laughing at his situation.

Wait? A gum tree?

Andy ripped back the zip, his heart pounding as red dust trickled in and landed on his face. He stood, brushing the dust from his eyes, as a sense of vertigo launched itself up his spine. He took one step from the swag and his eyes snapped open as he started to lean into a void.

Over a cliff.

Andy tottered on the balls of his feet, his arms windmilling to regain balance. He staggered away from a sharp edge where the rock stopped abruptly and the yawning distance began. He dropped to his knees, the terra-cotta rubble cracking under his weight. The whipping wind beat his ears in a constant thrumming as a flock of black birds swooped past his ears and dived over the edge. Low, squat mounds of thick, tinder-dry grass dotted the rock platform that sat between him and . . . oblivion.

Andy crawled to the rock's edge, cut away by years of weather and story, leading to a dead drop of five hundred feet. A winding ribbon of crystal-blue water shepherded by thick gum trees and large rocks seemed cut in two as if cleft by a giant sword. The sense of vertigo again mugged him, spinning his vision. His breath shallowed in an overwhelming sense of panic.

This wasn't the cliff he'd been lowered from earlier—that was a mere bump in the landscape compared to this height. And Sloaney had told him that cliff next to the water hole was the only one near the campsite.

Andy crawled back from the edge, throwing frantic glances left and right, scrambling to latch on to anything that made sense. His swag, into which he had commando-crawled to seek refuge from the whirling sandstorm, was the only thing that was recognizable. It sat on a small plateau of rock, his only company a tall gum tree that stretched over the river below, a couple of berry-laden bushes, and a pile of boulders reaching twenty feet into the air.

Another throaty laugh burst from the gum tree above him. The campsite was gone.

———

Andy's hoodie flew out of his swag, followed by his pillow, then his backpack. He had to find his phone. The wind tousled his hair and blew around the giant gum tree whose spindly limbs jutted at crazy angles over the cliff's edge, as if pointing to one of the many ways back. Or forward. Or anywhere.

The cliff's edge.

How did he get here? This had to be a prank. He'd slept so heavily that the others had bundled him into the four-wheel drive and left him in the middle of nowhere. No tire tracks, no footprints, or anything that would show which way the others had gone. This was punishment for forcing an intervention where one wasn't welcome. Why couldn't they understand that if he disappeared, then his problems would disappear with him?

Andy's fingers found the hard rectangle of his phone under his sleeping bag. It gave him two pieces of news he didn't want and couldn't face. His phone was almost dead, and it had no service. What had been a relief five minutes ago was now a problem. A big problem.

Andy scratched at his greasy hair as his lips curled with contempt. They wanted him to call out for help, and there was no way he was going to give them the pleasure. He breathed hard to regain control.

Eliza had been bugging Eddie to do a journey, and she was forcing him to deal with his issues her way, trying too hard to fix a problem she had no business meddling with. Lincoln would be in on it as well. But how did they get him away from the campsite? It had to be the bush food. Spiked. They had been insistent that he try the goanna and the damper. He shouldn't have caved and had that one bite.

Andy's frazzled nerves settled, but he wasn't going to play their game. They wanted him to cry out for help, but he would do this himself. So, what did Eddie say about these journeys of discovery? They started with a step into the desert and then a discovery of who you really were.

Andy brushed off the clothes now strewn with red Australian dirt and shuffled carefully to the cliff's edge. The thin river below wound its way on the path of least resistance to its destination. Beyond it, the ground swelled to rolling hills studded with rocky outcrops and patterns traced in the landscape like a giant had trailed a comb across them.

Instructions. Maybe they'd been left in his swag. Ten feet away the low-slung bushes rattled and shook. If they were trying to hide, they were doing a horrible job. The bush parted and a flickering tongue emerged, followed by a pointed leather nose and narrow, beady eyes. The lizard's sturdy body was covered with a taut hide and a long tail, sweeping aside handfuls of rubble and puffing dust into the air. Knee high to Andy, it was a good stone's throw from his swag, but sadly he couldn't throw a stone that far. His first challenge. They sent this prehistoric lizard to scare him. It was partially working.

Andy forced the nerves from his voice. "Hi, buddy."

The goanna cocked its head, its flicking tongue tasting the direction in which to charge.

Andy moved only his eyes. If it did charge, there was only one place to go.

The goanna lumbered toward him. Andy let out an involuntary scream and backed up to the gum tree, reaching for the lowest limb. The bark peeled away, and he staggered back with fists full of the flaking rough skin of the gum. The goanna was closing in.

Andy again grabbed for the limb, the smooth skin of this ancient tree now slipping under his fingers. He found some purchase and pulled himself off the ground. His feet dangled as the lizard slowed. It stood beneath him, eyeing him with suspicion, its serpent tongue flicking.

Andy's heart pounded in his chest and his ears. A tremor rippled through him, his limbs buzzing. He'd failed the first challenge, but he still hadn't called for help. *I will deal with this myself and not give you the satisfaction.* He could do this— all he had to do was chase away the goanna. He surveyed the area. A fallen limb rested against the trunk. That would do.

With an annoyed headshake, his attacker lumbered away

with its strange, swaying gait. Halfway to the bushes it turned and headed straight for Andy's backpack, nosed it open, and rummaged inside.

"Hey!" Andy's voice strained in the rapidly drying heat. "Hey!" His arm waving went unrewarded, but the path was now clear to the fallen limb. Andy landed with a thud, turning his ankle on the loose rocks. The goanna eyed him, a sliver of candy wrapper trailing from its mouth.

He lunged for the branch and, with a primal scream drawn from the depths of his very survival, ran at the prehistoric beast, waving his newly found weapon with gusto. The reptile gave a startled hiss and rushed into the only place it could find to hide. Andy's swag.

Andy skidded to a halt. Any instructions of what to do next now sat underneath a giant lizard, along with his hat, sunblock, glasses, and everything else he'd need. He reached for his backpack. At least he still had his water bottle, small as it was.

He fixed his eyes firmly on his adversary, the swag now still. A flickering in the corner of his eye grabbed his attention. Away from the cliff, a distant deep-red vein throbbed in the heat haze. That could be the dirt track they'd used to drop him off, and it wasn't too far away.

And there was a dust cloud heading toward him. They were coming back, and if he made good time, he could probably reach it. He would turn the tables and catch them unawares. And, holding the element of surprise, he would unload. On them all.

With one eye on his now-still swag, he hoisted the backpack onto his shoulder and jogged away from the cliff, grinning as he headed for the dust cloud.

FIFTEEN

Eliza's hot breath assaulted her senses into action. The claustrophobia from the green wall an inch from her face clawed at her neck as her mind slowly caught up with her body. Her shallow breaths lengthened as she centered herself, until the memory of last night crashed into her self-control. She was responsible for the intervention that had blown up in all their faces. At least Andy had found his way back. The slamming car door had told her as much.

The flashes of last night continued to fire. Andy, hooked not by the specter of drugs but gambling. And Lincoln, a lovesick old boyfriend stuck in the past, obsessed with a woman she used to be, and using her rejection as an excuse for ruining his life. There was no way she would be the rebound after a divorce. Still, she wouldn't let it spoil her time away. She had Bree and would leave Lincoln to deal with his issues.

Bree.

The betrayal from her old friend bit deep. She'd lied for years about an audition she'd never gone to. Eliza's mind raced ahead and she reined it in. Now wasn't the time to evaluate everything they'd shared, inspecting it for clues.

She gritted her teeth as her resolve hardened. This trip would still be significant, even if she had to experience it all by herself. She shuffled the memories and filed them away, but one card wouldn't fit. Part of her life *was* missing, and the missing part of the puzzle could be someone. But it definitely wasn't Lincoln.

She reached for her phone: 7:00 a.m. Hopefully the storm hadn't wrecked their campsite and whatever Eddie had in store for them today. The dust had blasted her swag for hours until she had given in to sleep.

Eliza listened intently for movement outside, to determine which conversation she would need to lead first. Silence. Being the first up was good. It would allow her to set the tone for the morning. Eliza wrenched open the zipper. The sky above her was baby blue, shining in unblemished perfection with not a hint of the previous night's maelstrom. She fully unzipped the swag, and as she got to her feet, something about the terrain jolted through her like an electric charge.

Her swag lay next to a graded road of dirt. A straight line of powdered red, the road fashion-runway straight to the horizon in both directions. Behind her, away from the road, nothing but empty plains. Across the road spinifex and scrubs dotted a landscape bereft of any signs of humanity.

The campsite was gone, and she was alone.

"Guys?" Eliza flicked through her options as she spun. "Eddie? Sloaney?"

Her analytical mind kicked into gear with the silence, turning over her situation until it found the most obvious solution. After telling her for two days that they wouldn't do a walkabout, Eddie had granted her wish, and this *had* to be the start of her journey of discovery.

The sense of dread that lapped at the edges of her self-control receded, replaced with the fierce determination that had carried her through life on her own, and that everyone in LA fashion knew was a trademark in itself.

She'd asked for a challenge, and she had one.

Her solitude took on a different dimension. She'd been left alone—that was good. She was with the only person she had trusted since college. The others didn't seem that keen on self-reflection and improvement anyway.

The sun flooded the landscape with an orange warmth. Eliza breathed in through her nose, letting it escape through her mouth as she stretched into it. Found center. Her drive now topped up, she loaded her backpack with the supplies she knew she needed—her phone, albeit still disconnected from the world, a towel, and a half-empty drink bottle she wished she'd filled last night. If only she'd been told. She would make do until she found the next checkpoint and the supplies certain to be there. There was no question she would beat the others back to the campsite. And she would make a point of beating Lincoln.

Discomfort. How deeply had she slept for them to bring her out here? Then a deeper layer of discomfort. What had they given her to make her sleep that deeply? The negativity rolled on.

Bree.

If they were all doing this spiritual trek, Eliza knew Bree wouldn't cope. Once again, responsibility fell to her—another series of jobs to do. She had to get back. Quickly.

Eliza craned her neck as she made her choice. "Let's do this." Turning left, she hiked along the road, head down, arms swinging, full of purpose.

"Challenge accepted!" She shouted over her shoulder to no one in particular, as she jammed down her Giants cap on her head. This was the reason she had come to Australia. *This* was the journey of discovery she'd been waiting for, not just for the past few months, but longer.

She turned toward the rising sun and headed toward it, a determined spring in her step.

The splinter's sting ripped through Lincoln's cheek as he woke with a start. His fingers caught the stout sliver of wood now embedded in his skin, but it was the cold wood underneath his other hand that shocked him fully into consciousness. He squinted in the dim light and shivered.

He sat bolt upright as his eyes scanned the room.

A room?

Torn lace curtains framed the source of the dim light—a window smeared with grime and dust. A solid mahogany desk sat against the wall, behind it an office chair of tubular steel and cracked burgundy leather. Empty shelves laced with cobwebs filled a corner, while a pin board spanned the wall's length, covered with paper held up by a constellation of gold and silver thumbtacks.

Lincoln rubbed his eyes as he spun full circle.

He was in a room?

He staggered to the window and pressed his face against it, his breath fogging the glass. The ground outside was covered in dark gravel before it ended suddenly. The land beyond was soft pink and red, a country waking and shaking off the night. Between the two extremes of color, a large sign of faded and chipped black letters on rust-spotted white steel proclaimed he was at Curdimurka Crossing. Next to it stood an unblinking red light encircled in black, with steel cables running down the length of its tall post. A railway signal.

Lincoln shook his head as he took in his surroundings. The platform's dark gravel extended in both directions. Next to the window was a bench, its dark-green paint peeling.

He was at a railway station, but how did he get here? And where was here?

Next to the window, a large door with thick, streaked, dark-green paint led outside. He leaned on the handle, firm and unyielding. He jiggled it—at first gently, then with a frustrated jerk. It wasn't budging.

The room contained two more doors. The first opened to a tiny room furnished with royal blue-and-white porcelain, a rust-stained washbasin, and a curtainless shower, steel loops hanging from a rusted railing. High above the shower, light streamed in through a tiny window encrusted with red dust.

Lincoln went to the basin and splashed chilled water onto his face, trying to wake up. Trying to force his brain to work. He swilled a mouthful of water and spat it into the sink. Stale. He stood back and stared into his own bloodshot eyes. What was going on?

A slow smile crept across his face. Despite Eddie's protestations, they were doing this self-discovery thing after all. Eliza had been granted her wish, and they needed to escape this room to prove themselves.

Eliza.

Lincoln gritted his teeth. He would escape from his room before she escaped hers, and he would be waiting casually outside her door while she staggered out. Then they'd resume their conversation from the night before.

He reemerged into the main room—the office of a stationmaster—and he grinned at the cornices at cameras that would surely be capturing his every move and frustration. He bowed theatrically. "Well done, everyone! I'm not sure how you got me here, but kudos on the drama."

Lincoln cracked his knuckles as he surveyed the room, looking for the easiest route of escape. The second door across the room gave in easily and opened to a waiting room—two rows of cracked, dusty leather seats, the elegant curve of empty mahogany coatracks, and a wooden brochure stand, bereft of paper. To his right a dozen metal lockers revealed part of their secrets, half the doors swung open. It was impressive—they'd really paid attention to detail.

Lincoln stood perfectly still in the center of the room, straining every fiber within him to hear the desperate shushing to keep the secret alive and the game afoot.

Silence.

It was time to shine, and it came with an added point to prove. Lincoln closed his eyes and rolled his neck. He strode back to the office and inspected the keyhole. It took a large key—he imagined it to be brass and with ornate metalwork—and it was in here. Somewhere.

He strode to the desk and pulled out a drawer, which screeched wood-on-wood but revealed nothing. Each drawer remained tight-lipped to a solution, except one unwilling to open. He slid his fingernails along the drawer's edge, but it was jammed shut. Something to come back to. He spun to the shelves, sweeping away cobwebs but finding nothing.

Lincoln charged into the waiting room, crawling across the wooden floorboards as he checked under the wooden-slatted seats, before he threw open the locker doors.

Nothing.

He raced back to the stationmaster's office. At the foot of the window sat two brass handles, their centers shiny with wear. He hooked his fingers under both, the brass cold to his touch. He lifted sharply and almost pulled his shoulders from their sockets. The window was unmoved.

Where would they hide the key? None of the floorboards were loose and there were no rugs under which it could hide.

The pin board. The overlapping papers of fading color fluttered at his approach. He moved his way down the wall. Train timetables, Curdimurka Crossing station circled on each of them. He lifted them, looking for a hidden key, but found only cork. Formal government letters and handwritten notes. Detailed props to this theatrical facade, but no key.

Lincoln stroked his chin as he evaluated his options. It wasn't going to be easy, but Eddie had said that a journey of discovery never was.

He looked back at the desk and its unyielding drawer.

He only needed to find a way to open it. He was sure it held the key.

The sibilant hiss dipped beneath the surface of Bree's light sleep and dragged up her consciousness with sharp fingertips. She slow-blinked herself awake. A hissing? What on earth was she dreaming about? The canvas around her feet crinkled, a rustling at the end of her swag, as terror coursed through her veins. The canvas dented above her toes. She wasn't dreaming.

The sweat beaded and ran down her temples in the dank, claustrophobic air of her sleeping quarters. She reeled in her panicked call to the others that would alarm this . . . She couldn't bring herself to say it. Snake. That would kill her in an instant if she made the slightest move.

Another soft hiss jerked her reflexes into action and she kicked out. The canvas popped, and the hissing stopped. Adrenaline replaced dread. She had to get out, and she only had a few seconds before the snake returned.

"Eddie! Sloaney!" Bree forced a flatness into her voice that belied her tremoring nerves. "Lincoln!"

No response, not even a whisper of wind.

"Lize?"

Nothing but cold silence.

"Okay, Breezy, you have to do this." She corralled her shallow breaths into order and forced them to sound off. "One." She clicked the zipper slowly open, one eye out for danger above. It was darker than the first morning. Colder too.

"Two." She gripped the zipper tight and pulled the canvas taut.

"Three!" She ripped the zipper open and jumped out of her swag, her ankles twisting on shifting pebbles. She spun full circle, tottering on unsteady feet as they sought purchase in a dry riverbed. In an instant the snake was forgotten. The stony floor was dotted with dry grass and clouds of insects buzzing around them. She was hemmed in by sheer red-and-ochre walls sliced from rock that stretched two hundred feet high, leaving a gap ten feet wide. The wall behind her was smooth, the one in front scored with diagonal scratches that ascended the rock, as if the passing of millennia here had not been gentle.

Her gaze drifted up. And up. At the halfway point of the ravine's dizzying climb, a lone gum tree reached out from the wall, its thin trunk emerging from a large crack, a hint of light peeking out from behind it. She continued her inspection up to the wedge of baby-blue sky framed by the blood-red cliff tops.

Two questions refused an easy answer: Where was she, and where was everyone else? This had to be a prank—probably Lincoln, as some kind of payback for last night for forcing him to reveal his secret to Eliza. Payback. It could be Andy, smarting over never being paid back for an audition that never took place. Guilt eased into her. She would have to make it up to him next time she saw him, somehow.

Then a third question hounded her: How on earth did they not wake her? Last night's dinner must have been spiked. That was the only way they could have done it.

Her tears made their regular appearance. Would Eliza have been part of this? All because Bree hadn't been honest about her audition?

The hissing began again. Faint. Close. It stopped. She backed into the solid rock wall. Her breaths came in short, shallow gasps, her frantic eyes roving to find the source. Her gaze was drawn to the swag and the mound of sand covering its end. With the tiniest puff of wind, one edge of the mound poured from the swag onto the rock beneath it, hissing as it hit and spread.

The sand made sense after the dust storm. Not much else did. This *had* to be a prank.

"Good one, guys." Her nervous laugh rebounded to her sharply from the cliff face.

"Eliza!"

The only response was her own, and it reached ears already full of her own thudding pulse.

At one end of the ravine, the rocks of the riverbed disappeared into a pool of lime-green water studded with boulders and a fallen tree. Random bubbles popped to the surface. Beyond the pool, rockfall reached halfway to the sky. She looked for a way through—the murky water gave nothing away, least of all its depth.

And it revealed she wasn't alone.

From the top of a lumpy rock in the middle of the pool, a coiled snake eyed her. Two vertical slashes stared her down amid dark-brown patches on a reddish-brown head, while its tongue lashed from what appeared to be a broad smile. Friendly and harmless, but only from a distance. Like a tax auditor.

This was no way out.

Bree's heart rose into her throat as she took two tentative steps back from the water. She scrambled back to the swag, her back to the danger. She shivered as a wedge-tailed eagle soared majestically into the ravine, its metallic screech bouncing down these impossibly high walls and enveloping her in its harsh echo.

Bree ducked by reflex as the eagle sailed the length of the ravine, then disappeared from view behind the lonely gum tree.

"Follow the riverbed out." She stumbled over the rocks, her arms outstretched for balance, and her eyes evaluated every shadow for danger. The pebbles gave way to solid rock slabs, scored and lined with fissures and cracks. The walls narrowed and she trailed her hands along them, at first with stretching fingertips, then with elbows tucked in. The air grew cold and stale as she approached another sheer rock wall. The ravine ended.

Panic set in as time slowed. They couldn't leave her down here with no way out.

She shivered as the cold snuck through the thin fabric of her T-shirt, and she trudged back along the scored rock floor to where the pebbles began and resumed her ginger scramble across shifting uncertainty.

Bree reached the swag and found her hoodie. She searched for her phone, but they'd taken it. The impossibility of her situation bit hard as she sank to her knees, and her heart sank with her hopes. She screamed at the sky two hundred feet above her.

Bree opened her eyes and saw the pulsing light behind the thin trunk of the lonely gum tree, clinging to impossible life almost through obstinence. The wall in front of her was jagged and cracked but it wasn't vertical. It leaned away with handholds and footholds. It was climbable.

There *was* a way out.

Up.

SIXTEEN

The crunch of the stones beneath Andy's boots beat a hypnotic tattoo that slowed his legs and time. Sweat basted him as he tripped over more of the same—ankle-high rocks and thick spinifex whipping his shins. His phone proclaimed he'd been walking through the low scrub for two hours and the dirt road was no closer.

The dust cloud had disappeared, along with his righteous anger—and his hope.

Andy swallowed hard, his throat like sandpaper, as desperation set in. In every direction was an endless sea of dry, red dirt pockmarked with stones and scattered boulders holding down the skin of this ancient country—the surface of Mars brought to Earth. He swooned in the glare of the blazing, burning sun and tried to get his bearings. Was the sun in front of him or behind?

Scuffed footprints in the red dirt led away. His own. The

heated air snatched his breath as he faced away from them and kept walking. The lure of his phone drew his hand to his pocket, before he jerked it away. He needed to conserve the all-but-dead battery for when he came back into range. Without it, he would be disconnected from everyone, and he needed a lifeline to the outside world. If he lost that, his desire to disappear for a while would become permanent.

Blotches of light exploded behind his eyes, fired by heat exhaustion and white-hot anger. Eliza and Lincoln had cooked this up with the tour guides. Some kind of macho *Survivor* thing he wasn't prepared for and didn't need. They were forcing him to discover himself, but he should have seen it coming—Eddie had said there were some surprises in store.

Andy's every nerve sizzled as his mind threw up fresh targets for his self-righteousness to take potshots. Bree for taking his money and lying to him about it. The net widened beyond those responsible for more than his current predicament—the horse that was a sure thing but ran last, almost to spite him. The Rams, who gave up an insurmountable lead and lost to the winless Giants. At home, in overtime. The bookies who ignored his impassioned appeals for a little more time or one final chance.

His pace quickened, the touchpaper of his adrenaline now lit. The rhythmic scratching of his boots marked time for the parade of the guilty, which now stretched to losses that were more than money. The jobs he'd run from due to the unshakeable suspicion that the missing money was down to him. The girlfriends who'd left after they'd discovered he'd borrowed more after not fulfilling his many promises of repayment. The apartment he'd loved in Cincinnati that he'd had to abandon in a midnight run from outstanding rent.

Andy approached a stand of gum trees, sprays of leaves studded with large white flowers. He leaned a cheek against a large gum, his soul singing in gratitude for the respite from the sun and the trunk's cool smoothness. He tipped his water bottle into a grateful mouth. One last dribble. He swallowed the tepid water and closed his eyes as the searing air sucked the water straight from his lungs.

The white flowers exploded into squawking life, as cockatoos flocked from the tree in a flapping, swooping mess of screeching and blinding white. Andy ducked and dropped to his knees, his head light, spinning and in turmoil. The tour guides had to come back, and the dirt road couldn't be much farther ahead.

His sweat dripped onto the dry earth like a ticking clock counting out measures of time he didn't have. As Andy swept the sweat-drenched strands of hair from his eyes he saw it. A tiny plume of dust. They were returning.

Andy forced himself to his feet, his calves twitching as he broke into a shambling, stumbling jog. He burst back into the burning sun, forcing his legs of jelly into action.

He couldn't miss this car. He just couldn't.

The office chair's rusted springs shrieked in protest as Lincoln threw himself back against the cracked seat back. The desk drawers sat upside down in front of him in an untidy pile, punishment for revealing nothing.

Except one. The bottom desk drawer sat defiantly in place, refusing to budge. It *had* to contain the key to get out.

Two hours, and he was no closer to getting that drawer open. He'd wracked his brain for any clues Eddie might have dangled. Any half-comment about a key or a throwaway line about escaping.

Lincoln leaped up to study the door. Again. It was painted shut, but the metal around the keyhole was shiny and worn, as if it could be opened. As if it *had* been opened. He dropped to his knees and peered into the keyhole, the light breeze brushing his face. A wind heating with the morning.

Lava bubbled within him. This was what they wanted him to do, and if they were watching, they'd take delight in his discomfort and his inability to solve what he would end up realizing was a simple problem. He stormed back to the desk and its recalcitrant drawer. He kicked at it and it didn't even shudder. But the pains shooting up his leg did.

He paced up and back along the pin board. Letters from the Railway Department—pleading letters of request stamped with rejection. Announcements of the closure of the line, sad but unavoidable. Papers filled with tiny fading numbers lined up in neat columns—departures and arrivals. Lincoln traced a finger along the line of numbers on the same row as Curdimurka Crossing Station. A dash. Trains didn't stop here. He glanced to the top of the timetable and found a number that slowed time. He traced a finger along the letters from the department.

They were dated fifteen years ago.

Lincoln's head swung around at the faint blaring sound beyond the locked door. Was that a train horn? He ground his teeth, needing to focus on the task at hand. He stepped along the wall, and none of the other papers revealed anything. Nothing but a series of letters from the Railway Department stamped in an angry red with letters that screamed the request had been rejected. Whatever the stationmaster had requested, he'd been knocked back. Hard.

Lincoln's frustration percolated, feeding the growing thoughts jostling for attention. Eliza's rejection. Again. Andy putting the blame on him for his problems rather than owning them. Bree's invasion of his privacy and ruining his chances with Eliza. He searched for answers—for meaning.

His stomach rumbled, and for a moment he drifted back to his regular table at The Daily Grill on Geary Street, a steaming lobster potpie under his nose. He hiked the steep incline to Nob Hill. A tiny part of him yearned to be home, even if it meant facing the army of divorce lawyers waiting for him, legal guns drawn.

The mere thought of Dianne's letter stabbed him into action. He shot to his feet and wrapped both hands around the door handle—jimmying it, then jerking it harder and harder hoping to force it open. He threw his shoulder into the peeling wood. *"Anybody?"*

Lincoln charged back into the waiting room. He flung open the already-open locker doors, their metallic banging swamping the small room. He sank to his knees, the last of the echoes ringing in his ears.

There was another sound. Something soft.

Beyond the door.

Someone was here.

Lincoln strained to hear it. Definitely footsteps. He raced back to the window but saw nothing but the railway station sign, now casting shadows across the platform. The railway signal still showed red.

His ragged breath fogged the window as he pounded on it, and it shuddered under his attack. A way out presented itself. He rushed to the desk and lifted the office chair, the heavy steel cold in his hands. He ran with a scream and hurled the chair at the glass.

The chair bounced off the window with a sharp clang, and he scrambled to one side to avoid it on the rebound. He stood blinking as the glass shuddered and then stopped. Lincoln kicked against the door, and another piercing jolt shuddered up his leg. He slid to the floor, his will leaking from him.

The padding sounded again. Footsteps, light and—to an ear well-trained in the art of waiting for a woman to arrive—with the slightest hint of heels. Now he was hearing things.

A throat cleared from behind the door. A polite clearing, then a sigh.

Lincoln peered through the keyhole. No one was there, but the breeze delivered a heady waft of perfume—an exotic mix of cinnamon and rose, tree bark and rammed earth. He pressed his cheek to the window, trying to see as far down the platform as the glass would allow.

On the bench brown legs were uncrossed, then recrossed. Lincoln's gaze started with the white sandal straps and roamed up shapely calves to a white-dotted-and-handprint-patterned dress.

The woman from the airport.

———

The light blurred halfway up the rock wall, in and out of focus as Bree blinked away jet lag and emotion. The light could only mean one thing. The ravine had another entrance. There was a way out. She wouldn't have to climb the dizzying heights of the whole wall.

The voices raged inside her. The ones who always doubted

her; the ones Sam had tangled with over the years. The sting-ing rebuke of fear, this time sneering with a reminder of her hatred of heights. The warmth of Sam's voice encouraging her that she was good enough to overcome anything. The barman at The Second Fiddle on Broadway telling her she was nothing but another dime-a-dozen singer with a guitar. Her girls cheering at her impromptu kitchen table concert. The head of the recording studio in Nashville switching off her demo with a snarl that he was hearing nothing special.

In each of these exchanges she sat silent on the sidelines—like she always did—unable to speak, unable to defend her-self. The voices continued, as she waited for the one voice that always came over the top. The one that had so shattered her self-confidence that it would never be any more than a loose collection of broken pieces.

The sobs came freely as she rocked back and forth on her swag, hugging her legs for comfort as much as warmth. She trailed her gaze up the wall, following a crack in the rock that led to a flat section, then another crack with places for her hands and feet. There was a definite path she could climb, but she couldn't do it. She wouldn't make it.

Bree jammed her eyes shut to drown out the voices as a familiar voice came to her aid. Her beloved Sam. Knowing she could do this. Knowing she had it in her. Her fragile, fleeting courage sprouted with the watering of his encourage-ment. Then, as if sensing her confidence rising, the voices were back. She was no good at music. She would never be good enough to achieve her dream. There was no future in music and a girl like her would never survive in New York.

A strong voice flooded her with comfort. Sam.

"You can do this, Breezy. We need you to do this."

She felt sure Sam was in the ravine with her. The fear took one last swing—pointing out the impossibility and the certainty of doom. But Sam's voice wouldn't be denied, and Bree now heard it on the outside as much as the inside.

"We believe in you, Bree. You can do this."

She looked up the ravine wall and saw a ridge, about half-way to the light emanating from the cave. She could rest there. She didn't have to go all the way, not at first.

After a single, weak breath, Bree banished the voices. The pebbles beneath her shaking feet rattled her nerves as she stood. She hitched her backpack higher on her shoulders, and a sense of vertigo crawled up her spine as she wrestled two handholds and placed a tentative toe in a crevice.

She could do this.

With her heart in her mouth, she lifted her first foot. The rock felt cool and almost soft under her hand. One slow foot after another, one slow handhold after another. She scaled her way up the diagonal crack, the tender skin of her hands scuffing on the rough rock, her toes trying to grasp the ravine wall through the soles of her shoes.

Eyes front.

She inched higher, each handhold pressing into soft flesh, her breath coming in jagged waves, her head spinning.

She stopped to rest her screaming arms. Even thinking about the word *down* was too much. She flicked a glance below and her vertigo mugged her. Her vision clouded, dizziness swept through her as sweat now poured down her neck, pooling at the small of her back. She jammed her eyes shut to regain her composure.

Bree reached for another handhold, the sweaty sheen on her hands forcing her to lose her grip. She screamed as she started to slide down the ravine wall. Her hands scrambled for something—anything—to save herself, her toes kicking to find purchase on rocks sharpened by millennia of wind and rain that would slice her in two if she fell.

With a jolt her toes found a crevice and she stopped her slide, her pulse thumping in her ears. Bree's body was wracked with sobs, numbed by draining adrenaline. Exhaustion. Confusion. And fear.

The light from the cave now flickered and brightened. She had to go back to where she came from. The light from above was her salvation.

But also from above a voice drifted down to her. A voice impossible to silence. Moving away from home hadn't put enough distance between her and the sniper's nest. Her mother's voice had simply taken up residence in her head, a roommate for her self-doubt.

"You can't do this. You won't do this. You never do."

Bree closed her eyes again as the video message from the plane replayed itself on the cinema of her mind. Sam and the girls. Her three reasons to get out of here.

She *had* to do this.

———

Eliza's enthusiasm leaked away with every trudging step. Her shoes sunk deep into the squeaking dirt as she trekked on, her shoulders sinking farther with each glance at a horizon that was getting no closer. She swept away the flies as the thought buzzed around her again, as it had for the past two hours.

I should have gone the other way.

Eliza's finely honed intuition had let her down, and the cost was looming as more than the chance of victory. She reached for her drink bottle, pointlessly. It had given up the last of its water an hour ago, when her shoulders were back and her confidence in finding supplies bounced along with the spring in her step. Now twinges of fear and doubt creaked within her. She pushed them down with a controlling hand, summoned energy into her twitching legs, and charged on.

This wasn't her fault. But now that she was hours into this trek, there was no turning back. Something had to appear. It had to. Unless she found shelter quickly, *when* she got back might become *if* she got back. Difficult would shift to impossible. And without water, it would move from impossible to inevitable.

The questions remained unanswered with no one to even pose them to. Surely the tour group wouldn't leave a tourist out here with no water. Someone had to be tracking her progress and reporting back to the campsite.

Unless . . .

Her trudging shoes scuffed on as Eliza fought to quell the doubt. Deep in thought, Eliza's toe caught a dip in the track and she lost the battle with balance. The dirt puffed around her hands as she landed hard.

Pain shot up her forearms as she slowly raised her eyes. Two feet ahead of her the points of a scorpion's pincers eased open as its tail uncoiled. The creature scuttled forward and Eliza backed away from the danger, one eye on the tiny creature as she scrambled to her feet. She ran wide of the scorpion, carried by the flood of negativity and fury that coursed through her. The tour company—for all its down-home charm and Steve Irwin-ness—was a backyard operation.

Eliza scanned her memory for every interaction with Eddie and Sloaney, evaluating them for clues that she should have seen this coming. From their website to the ride to the campsite to their activities the previous day, her memory gave up nothing, except identify the only other person possibly at fault.

The man who'd booked a tour with a company clearly unqualified to handle it.

She powered on—she had to be positive. Her wits needed to be about her, not lost in a blame game she couldn't afford to play. Not yet at least.

A light wind picked up and whipped around her. Cooling her head. Bringing relief and the realization: She was being tested. Stretched. Dragged out of her comfort zone. This was actually what she wanted.

Calmness filtered back in as the pieces fell into place. This was hard because it was supposed to be hard. She was being stripped away, and she would push through it. This was her challenge and she would overcome it.

She checked her phone—disconnected with the world, it was now just a flat clock in her pocket. Midday. She trudged on. Head down. Bringing her thoughts back from the brink.

Eliza's soaked sleeve absorbed another browful of sweat. The wind lifted, struggling to move the greasy strands of hair pasted to her forehead. A shape materialized in the distance. Tall, thin. A structure.

She'd made it. This had to be a checkpoint in this game of survival, and it vindicated her decision. Her self-confidence tipped its hat right again. She broke into a jog as the detail of the shape filled in. A windmill, next to a squat water tank, next to a traffic sign—a black cross on a yellow diamond, high above the road on a thin pole. A crossroads. Finally, she had options.

Eliza rushed to the shade cast by the windmill, her skin almost singing at being out of the singeing sun. She surveyed the rainwater tank, rusted holes peppering its corrugated, round surface above a tap that had to be red hot in this burning sun. She wrapped a sleeve around her hand as she turned the tap, her water bottle waiting gratefully below it.

She whooped as the first dribble of water brought a wash of great relief, but it was fleeting. After a trickle, the water ran dry. Nevertheless, her water bottle was no longer empty. She gratefully chugged at the water, the tangy mustiness not quenching only her thirst but also her rising unease.

The squat windmill's blades sat unmoving in the super-heated air. If this was a checkpoint, there had to be a clue somewhere. She circled the water tank, which revealed nothing but disappointment seeping from rusting holes. The road sign was just scratches with rust licking at its edges.

Dirt roads to her left and right, copy-and-pastes of the road stretching in front of her and the one she'd traveled for hours. Each corner held its secrets—no tire marks, evidence of the direction the Outback Tours vehicle had taken after dropping her off. She looked back at the windmill. There was only one thing left to do.

She wrapped her hands in her sleeves and clambered up the steel bars. The heat pulsated through the thin, damp fabric, threatening to blister overheated skin. She reached the blades and scanned the horizon. In one direction a dirt road arrowed into the heat's distant haze. In the other a mirror of the first. There was nothing else to see.

Eliza stifled an anguished scream and pounded her fists on the blade's searing metal. She wiped away the sweat from her eyes and slowed her breathing, reining in runaway emotions that never were helpful.

She needed to center herself. She set her jaw and put her faith in the only person she could trust. Herself. She slid back in the driver's seat of her life and made a focused choice. Straight ahead was as good a direction as any. She'd put miles between her and where she woke up.

As she hitched her backpack higher and charged across the crossroad, the usual peace that came with her decisiveness wavered. Doubt reared its head again. The mind that confidently proceeded across the intersection was the same one that turned left to begin her journey. She batted it away. Doubt was more than useless out here.

It was dangerous.

SEVENTEEN

Andy staggered toward the mushrooming dust plume, his body imploring him for relief as the sun's baking heat hit its zenith.

A familiar tone burst from Andy's pocket and he all but cried. He was back in cell phone range, and they must have seen him. They were calling with instructions of where to meet the Outback Tours four-wheel drive stocked with water, food, and profuse apologies.

Andy whipped out his phone. The message was curt. Where are you?

I'm in the middle of nowhere thanks to you idiots.

He stared hard at the screen. The number was familiar. Very familiar. And a chill of dread skittered through him.

The number belonged to his bookie.

His phone beeped again. And where is my $100k?

Andy glanced at the top corner of the screen, where the rest of the world used to be, but something was still missing.

Numbing shock buckled his knees. There were no bars showing his connection to the outside world. Two words. *No Service.*

His breathing grew ragged as his mind spun. They had to be old messages, but how could—?

The roar of an engine buzzed to him from the horizon. Andy dug deep into a well of resources he was sure he had almost tapped out. His throat burned, and his muscles cramped, and the uneven crunching under his feet sped up. The black of the Outback Tours four-wheel drive approached and Andy stumbled, hands out to save himself from face-planting in the dirt. They were only a half mile away.

"Hey!" Andy's voice eked out of him in a dusty croak as he waved frantically.

The four-wheel drive didn't slow.

"Hey!" Andy lumbered toward the road, his thick legs now overheated, malfunctioning pistons. The engine's roar was joined by the pinging stones kicked up by the tires. Only a hundred yards away.

He wasn't going to make it. Andy skidded to a halt, his arms thrown into the air, his phone flying with it. *"Hey!"*

The four-wheel drive sailed past, veered around a large gum tree that reached majestically into the sky, and disappeared behind a large pile of boulders.

The scream that burst from Andy was drawn from the black depths of a lost last chance. A beeping cut through a cloud of the choking dust and his hope rose. They must have heard him and were driving back. He coughed as he stumbled into the dust cloud. Another beep guided him to where his cell phone had landed. A message now appeared under the spiderwebbed glass of the now-shattered screen.

It wasn't from Outback Tours.

Where's our 50k Andy?

He sunk to his knees, sobs wracking him as he sucked in dust-laden oxygen through a tinder-dry throat. Head bowed, he buried his fingers in the burning ground. This was a different phone number. But it was still a bookmaker. Another one.

Andy couldn't stop his eyes from roving to the top of the screen. The same two words that should have kept out those chasing him were now letting them through. *No Service.* How were these old messages appearing?

The phone beeped in his hand. Joey Waterhouse always collects, and I will find you Andy.

Joey Waterhouse.

Andy froze as the dust cloud dispersed, giving way to the burning sun. Two earth-shattering revelations collided head-on in the middle of his thinking. This wasn't an old message. This was a new phone he'd bought in the midnight rush from Cincinnati, so Joey couldn't have his number. His dripping sweat peppered the ground as a voice floated toward him on a gust of wind.

Wait . . . Was that—? The four-wheel drive must have stopped, and they were on foot looking for him. Andy staggered in a light-headed half-walk, half-jog toward the gum tree as he heard the voice again. Male. Flat. Australian. But this voice was harsh—it didn't carry Eddie's soft-spoken tones or the undercurrent of Sloaney's permanent grin.

Andy squinted before he rubbed his eyes. In the gum tree's shade sat a chocolate-brown leather sofa behind a long, low mahogany coffee table. Andy squinted harder as his mind did backflips.

The voice drifted out again from behind the tree. It was followed by a man who wasn't part of his tour group, but one he was sure he'd seen before.

———

Lincoln's knuckles stung as they rapped urgently on the window. The woman's legs remained unmoving, as the ruffle of a breeze played with the hem of her dress. His rap became an insistent knock, but the only other sound that reached Lincoln's ears was the grumble of an ignored stomach.

He thumped out his frustration on the door with his fist. "Hello?"

He stood back, the loud silence wrapping itself around each labored breath. The voice that came to him through the door dripped with an enchanting softness. "Hello?"

Oh thank goodness. "Hello! I'm stuck in here and the door is jammed. Could you help me?"

"Who are you?"

"I'm a tourist from the USA, and I've been separated from my tour group."

The woman's voice almost drowned in dark honey. "Where are they?"

"I don't know. I believe they might be back at the campsite."

"How did you get here?" Curiosity surfed on the gentle, flat cadence of her accent.

A question without an easy answer. "Could you try the door for me? Please?"

The door handle jiggled and stopped. "How do I know you are who you say you are?"

Lincoln exhaled hard. Why couldn't she try the door? "It appears someone has locked me in here, and I need your help."

"What type of person would lock you in?"

"I wish I knew."

"Better yet, what type of person are you that would need to be locked in?"

The strain of hours of fruitless searching for answers only for the solution to remain an infuriating few inches away cracked Lincoln's voice. "What can I do to show you I'm not a threat?" He strode to the window and threw out his hands. *"Please?"*

Raven hair flecked with gold appeared at the window's edge, followed by chocolate skin, furrowed eyebrows escorted by crow's-feet around her eyes, and a shy smile adorned with red lipstick. Her timeless beauty cut down his irritation. The woman faced him through the glass, studying him up and down. She gave a slow nod. "Okay."

"Could you please try the handle?"

She disappeared from view again, and the handle jiggled. "I can turn the handle from here, but it feels like it's locked from the inside. Don't you have a key?"

Lincoln swallowed a growl. "Don't you think if I had a key I would have used it by now?"

The young woman reappeared at the window and lowered her eyes, before she drilled her gaze into him. A knowing gaze. "I don't know. Would you?"

"Well, could you call someone for me?"

She shrugged. "There's no coverage out here. If there were, wouldn't you have called by now?"

A fair question.

She gazed down the platform before she again fixed him with a lingering look. "Could you try again to let me in? It's getting quite warm out here, and I'd like to wait inside."

Lincoln shook his head. "I've tried the door."

Her eyes softened. "Please, could you let me in?"

With a sharp shake of his head, Lincoln moved back to the door and gripped the handle that had refused to cooperate a dozen times already. It was warm, as if the morning sun had kissed it on its early rise. He turned hard, expecting nothing.

But he got something.

The handle eased, throwing him off balance, and he pulled open the door. The woman stood in front of him, a figure of exotic elegance, the handprint dress clinging to her all the way beyond her knees. A battered brown suitcase sat by her side. She held out her hand. "Thank you so much. I'm Alinta."

Her skin was the softest he'd ever felt and smelled of sandalwood and rain. He held the handshake for a moment too long as he looked into eyes that carried both the wisdom of age and the beauty of youth. Somehow. "Lincoln."

Alinta glided past him into the station building. Lincoln leaned out the door and glanced down the platform. No one was around, and in every direction beyond the platform was more of the same. Low-slung brush in a world where the early morning pink had gearshifted to reddish brown.

He ran down the platform into sunlight already burning the asphalt and threw himself on the chain-link fence at its end. Two thick steel tracks—partly buried under a fine red powder, thousands of years of the country's heart ground into dust—perched on splintered ties that had succumbed to years of weather. The pockmarked steel, riveted to the ground by rusted iron bolts as thick as his fist, stretched into the distance in a wavy parallel, across flat land dotted by wispy dry grass and desperate shrubs. But twenty yards along the line, crisscrossed steel beams blocked the tracks—a buffer stop lashed to the line by thick steel cables.

Lincoln ran to the platform's edge to see from where the rusted tracks had come. Nowhere. They shimmered away from him, took a right-hand bend, and then reached for the other horizon.

Behind the station was more of the same, and a dirt road free from tire tracks.

There was not a hint of where this woman had come from.

EIGHTEEN

Bree's muscles screamed as she reached for another hand-hold. She lifted a leg deadened with unfamiliar activity and resumed her slow climb. Foothold. Handhold. Foothold. Handhold. Fingers feeling for security. Toes searching for purchase. Arms screaming for rest.

She leaned into the wall, grateful for its gentle incline. The rock cut into her cheek and her legs quivered as she jammed her toes farther into the wall.

"Okay, Breezy, you have to do this."

Her fingers found a handhold wider than others. Deeper. The ledge. Respite was now within arm's reach. She patted the ledge, gripping it as she threw a leg up, pulling herself onto the thin strip of rock, her arms and legs sagging at the release from her weight. She lay back and stared at the gum tree, now only twenty feet above her.

Her stomach raged, forcing her thoughts back to home, drawing her to Jack's Bar-B-Que on Broadway. What she would give to be in an upstairs booth—the windows open and music wafting up from the street. She could almost smell the ribs, the mac and cheese, and the cornbread; taste the crunch of the green beans and the tang of the coleslaw. And the laughter of Sam finishing the girls' meals. Again.

Bree surveyed the ravine from her new vantage point. The rock in the middle of the lime-green water was now empty. She forced away the creeping image of the snake, replacing it with Emily and Imogen, their cowboy boots scuffing during their impromptu ballet. Beyond the boulders the ravine opened out to a land of nothing but dunes of red and knee-high shrubs. None of it was familiar. Once she got out of the ravine, she would need to find the campsite.

Fatigue settled into her limbs and her eyes grew heavy. The cast of cutting voices stormed back in a growing cacophony. Condemning. Labeling. Weakening. Then they stepped aside for their leader, who matter-of-factly poked at her flaws with precision. *Give it to me. There's no point in you even trying. You will never be able to do this on your own.*

But Sam's voice didn't rise to her defense against her mother. Instead a thin voice emerged. Her own.

Yes I will.

"You never make the right choices." Her mother's voice wouldn't be denied.

On the wall opposite, the smooth surface—without handholds—shone as the sun reached high over the ravine and flooded her with warmth. With self-confidence. *I did this time.*

The internal critic—the loudest of the voices who had cut away at her for years—offered a final pronouncement. *"You always need me to finish things you start, Bree."*

No I don't, Mom.

Bree forced a mental replay of her family's video. They needed her. She rose on unsteady feet, filled with righteous indignation. She could do this. She breathed hard and reached for her water bottle, relishing the cold flood that rippled through her.

She slowly leaned over the ledge's edge, a cautioned glance at the distance she'd come. It was farther than the distance left.

Bree slung the backpack and reached for another handhold, another toehold—her complete focus on the gum tree as it reared another foot closer. She reined in her rampant breathing and a singular thought stunned her in the absence of the usual dread over a taken risk. *Am I enjoying this?*

Bree smiled as she jammed her toes into a crack and pushed up. Her toes slipped out of a crack not as deep as it needed to be. She clung to the wall by her fingertips, her foot stabbing at the wall. Her arms screamed as her other foot lost its purchase and swung in the void. Her heart pounded as she peered down at the ledge, only a few feet below, but her hands held the rock in an iron grip.

The quiver in her arms graduated into an uncontrollable shake that threatened to vibrate her back to the ravine floor, a hundred feet below. The vertigo again tried to mug her and she battled for control. She couldn't climb this far again.

She had to let go. She had to do this for Sam and the girls. She had to do this for herself.

Her clawed fingers refused to cooperate as acid burned through her arms. She pried one finger from the rock and eased her thumb away. The grip on her other hand relaxed and she gently let go, her heart in her throat, sliding back down to the ledge, her hands guiding her descent.

Three feet . . .

Two feet . . .

Bree reached for another handhold to steady the pace of her descent and the rock sliced into the soft pad of her palm at the base of a finger. With a soft pat her feet touched down on the ledge and she stood, wringing her stinging hand, the blood joining her sweat in drips on the ledge. Tears threatened to unleash as she held the sliced skin of her finger together.

Her mother was triumphant. *"I told you so."* Bree snapped a look at the ravine wall opposite, convinced the voice was aiming at her from there.

A second voice seemed to join her in the ravine. Sam. *"You can do this, Breezy."*

Bree stared up at the gum tree. "I *can* do this."

"You'll never make it." Her mother's comment about a fledgling music career came back to her.

Bree screamed at the sky, "I WILL MAKE IT."

She shook her head to stop the beatdown, but this time her voice was not drowned out by Sam or even her own thin voice.

She heard the tapping of sticks. Coming down to her from above.

Bree leaned out from the ledge. "Hello?"

The sticks tapped louder, an insistent rhythm, their sharp clicks arrowing back at Bree from around the ravine.

"Hello?"

The tapping was joined by a guttural growl, a low hum that seemed to be drawing a vibration from deep within the earth. A voice.

Bree squinted into the blue. "Eddie? Is anybody up there?"

The music continued, and the light from the cave flickered.

Salvation. She took a deep breath and studied the palm of her hand. For all its blood, the cut was now clean, raw, and cold in the open air. She took another tentative glance to the ravine floor and back up to the gum tree. She had made it this far. She could do this.

Bree's confidence tiptoed back as she ascended, her trust in the wall shaken enough to proceed with more caution. She grimaced at the sharp, stabbing pain in her finger.

Hand-over-hand, her feet finding nooks, she ascended.

The gum tree was five feet away, and the space behind them diminished as she inched closer. The humming and clicking poured from the cave, washing her in the one thing in life that spoke to her. She headed toward the music as this clicking beat for the ancient instrument drew her in. Drew her up. Gave her a metronome to follow.

Two handholds. Just two handholds. The sharp rock threatened her fingers again as her deadened arms tremored. "Hey! Down here!" Bree's voice gave out as the tapping's volume rose again. She homed in on it. Music always had been her salvation.

One last handhold. With one final push on stiffening legs, her fingers gripped the gum tree's thick, ropelike roots that squirreled deep into the rock. Her other hand reached for the ledge and patted the rock. It was cold. And a breeze caressed her knuckles.

The tapping sticks grew in pace. She swung her leg onto the ledge and, with one almighty scream, vaulted onto it.

And as she lay on her back on the cool rock of the cave floor, a waft of damp air drifting over her, her heart pounding and her finger throbbing, the rhythmic tapping stopped.

———

A crow's mournful, mocking caw fluttered down to Eliza as the bird swooped on the growing breeze. Another two hours of nothing but a straight road. Another two hours of baking in the harsh sun, her will evaporating. She slathered on another layer of sunblock, but still she burned and she breathed deep to center herself. It took more than the usual six breaths.

The first doubts had started their cancerous growth twenty minutes from the intersection, and they were eating her self-confidence alive.

A rush of wind picked up, buffeting her. She walked backward to see the track now shrouded in dust. At least she wasn't back there anymore, but the dust was heading for her. The memory of the storm at their campsite flared back to life. She would need shelter, but there was nowhere to hide out here. She had no idea where here was, and in that moment, she would take the CEO job if it meant she could step into a four-wheel drive or even be handed a glass of water. The disappointment rose in her as she leaned toward escape rather than achievement. She was better than this.

Fine dirt stung her calves as she broke into a jog. The wind lifted her onto her toes, carrying her along the road. A shape appeared next to the track, two hundred yards away. A feature on an otherwise featureless landscape. Low and sturdy. A checkpoint, or at the very least somewhere to hide.

The wind ratcheted up further, now howling and pushing her hard. Head down, she covered her eyes from the swirling dust, focusing on the ground two steps ahead. A quick squint. The shape looked like the box of supplies Sloaney had placed in their campsite. She had found water and food and somewhere to wait out this dust storm.

Her cautious jog slowed as her feet throbbed and slid inside her shoes, blisters beneath her skin plotting their revenge. Her tongue grew dry at the promise of water. Head down, she pushed on. Another cautious glance. The shape was only fifty yards away. Long, thin, and green.

A swag. She was not alone.

They'd dropped off one of her colleagues along the journey as well, and that meant her friends were out here too. Her heart leaped with the hint of hope she wasn't on her own.

"Bree! Andy! Lincoln!" She ran along the track, her shouts swallowed by the swirling wind, her voice dry and cracking as the dust coated it.

She closed in on the swag as small pebbles pinged her legs, the dirt slashing at her shins.

Twenty yards.

Ten.

She sprinted the final distance to the swag and dived in, then zipped it up around her. Her heart pounded hard, and her hot, shallow breath bounced back at her from green canvas that buckled and bent in the howling wind and the blasting sand.

She lay back, grateful for the shelter Eddie and Sloaney had left. Sweat flowed down her face in this overheated canvas coffin. She had to outlast the storm, then she would reemerge and press on.

Supplies.

Her fingers rummaged around the swag, looking for the supplies that their guides should have provided. Her fingers found something hard and round. Round balls of wood and rough twine. It couldn't be. Her fingers trembled as she brought the item to her eyes, and her resolve cracked down the middle. No! The bracelet gift for Emily's auntie Lize.

After five hours of walking a dirt road in a straight line, she had found the swag in which she'd woken.

She was back to where she started.

NINETEEN

G 'day, mate."

Two words—the first Andy had heard all day outside his head. From behind the thick, mottled gum tree, corks jumped and swayed from a battered hat as a heavyset man waved a thick, hairy arm. Dark-blue tank top and brown shorts. He grinned as he plopped onto the leather sofa, stretched extravagantly, and crossed his stained beige work boots on the coffee table.

Andy's mind refused to work. "Who—?"

The man leaped to his feet and rushed across to him, his grease-stained hand outstretched. "I'm sorry, mate. How rude. Smithy."

"Smithy?" Andy's voice hissed out in a rasp.

"Bumped into you at the airport, didn't I?" Smithy pumped Andy's hand. The waft of aftershave, grease, and sweat was overpowering. "You look parched, mate! We need to get you inside and get a drink into ya." He threw an arm around Andy and walked him down the dirt track toward the large rise, which seemed to force the road around it, bending it to its will.

One of Smithy's words snagged in Andy's tangled thinking. "Inside?"

Smithy chuckled. "Yeah, mate, can't get a drink out here, can ya? Hot today, isn't it? So how did you get here?"

Andy grasped for something—anything—that made sense. Smithy, who appeared out of nowhere. A sofa and a coffee table under a gum tree. A disconnected phone receiving messages. He made his way around the bend in the road, and his brain threw up its hands and put in for vacation leave.

A building stood proudly in the dust. It had a long, corrugated iron roof, white with age and heat damage, propped up by white posts with ornate webs of steelwork spanning between them. Beneath it a verandah shaded dusty windows, a long wooden railing underlining them. A spring-loaded screen door hung slightly off its hinges and sat under a sign that proclaimed the entrance to the Front Bar, flanked by large, stylized photos of drinks with hunks of ice. The bottom third of the building was dusted in the red heart of the country, and a thick wooden sign swung in the heated breeze: *Come inside, we have what you need.*

"What is this place?"

Smithy stomped up the wooden steps, and the screen door shrieked as he held it open. "It's a pub. Can tell you're not from around here."

Splinters caught Andy's hot palms as he reached for the handrail. The glorious shade swept over him, and a blast of cool air wrapped him in its embrace. Andy walked into a wall of laughs and music. The pub was full, some people leaning against the bar, others standing around high tables laughing as they raised their glasses. Posters plastered the walls—frosty beer glasses and wide smiles. Framed photographs of great sporting moments—horses midstride at the finish line, footballers seated on the shoulders of cheering teammates, a gold medal pressed to an athlete's puckered lips.

Along the ceiling a line of flags fluttered in the cool, crisp air, leading to the far corner where a chunky box of a television played grainy music videos, its picture flickering under hazy snow. Beneath it, a group of men in checked shirts and wide-brimmed hats flipped coins into the air and thrust cash at each other. Floating over the music and noise, a heady aroma of food wafted toward him.

Smithy elbowed his way through the crowd and leaned against the bar. "A drink for my friend and I, and something to eat, please."

A thick-set barman, coils of steel-wool gray bursting from the top of his T-shirt, waddled toward them. He splayed chunky fingers on the countertop like a sprinter awaiting the starter's pistol as he towered over Smithy. "What will you have?"

Smithy pulled out a battered leather wallet. "I'm down to my last twenty, so what will that get me and my friend?"

The barman glanced at the chalk-scrawled menu board leaning against shelves of bottles and glasses, below a series of hats nailed to the wall in a neat line. "We'll see what we can do. Grab a seat." He snatched the orange note from Smithy's wallet and reached for a glass.

Andy slipped alongside Smithy, his body temperature resuming normal transmission. Unexplainable or not, he would rather be here than staggering around in the sun. A tanned, sinewy man in a blue-, red-, and yellow-striped sweater slopped amber liquid from two glasses held high as he maneuvered around Andy. "Coming through, mate."

A barmaid in a tied-off checked shirt ushered them to a table as a familiar song drifted across the bar from a juke-box against the far wall. Andy chuckled. Even an American could recognize the jaunty flute line of Men At Work's "Down Under." The barmaid placed two cardboard coasters in front of them and a basket cradling two tiny bread rolls topped with the smallest slivers of butter. "Hop in."

Smithy yawned hard. "Andy, you're lucky I found you when I did. How did you get out here?"

Where had all these people come from? Sweaty T-shirts and long shorts, light dresses pasted onto thin frames with sweat. A loud cheer burst from the corner as money changed hands and two copper coins were again flung into the air by a man in a large brown hat holding a large wooden paddle. "Two heads. Come in spinner!"

Andy smeared butter onto a roll and jammed it whole into his mouth. His body flooded with the crunch of crust and the sweetness of dairy. In seconds the roll was gone.

The savory, heavy aroma of deep frying assaulted Andy. The sweetness of bubbling sauces. His stomach joined the conversation with a low grumble, and he turned to Smithy. "I would have faded away without your help."

"I think you're going to need my help beyond whatever that barmaid brings back."

Another cheer burst from the corner. Fists full of purple, blue, and orange notes and two tiny coins glinted in sunlight streaming through the window. "Two tails. Come in spinner!" A hypnotic blur of copper streaks. The tiniest craving awoke in the base of his brain and it had nothing to do with the food.

Across the table his new friend's brow furrowed. "I would advise against that."

Her tray held high, the barmaid pushed through the crowd. She put down two tall, frosty glasses of clear, bubbling liquid, condensation running down their sides. Andy sighed as the ice clinked in the glass and raised it to his lips. It was sweet, with a light, bitter fizz, and the first mouthful slid down his throat.

The barmaid placed a tiny plate in front of each of them containing a small pie, no bigger than Andy's fist. "Gentlemen, this is what twenty bucks gets you." She winked at Andy.

Andy picked up the pastry and breathed deep, savoring the smell. In two bites it was gone.

Another glint from the corner. "Two tails!" Fistfuls of cash were again exchanged. The coins were flung into the air by the man in the wide brown hat, but Andy was no longer interested in him or his coins. His eyes were on the cash, and his mind turned over ways he could get some.

―――

The squeaking skid of Lincoln's running shoes echoed through the stationmaster's office after his fruitless search for a key found more questions than answers. And Alinta was gone.

Had she really been here? "Alinta?"

"Yes?" Sweetness floated from the waiting room.

Lincoln sprinted toward her voice. She sat quietly on cracked leather, ruby-red nail polish punctuating her neatly folded hands. He was assaulted by a heady cloud of perfume—an intoxicating mix of blossom and earth. The tiniest crow's-feet creasing the corners of her eyes held a knowing look—he could not even guess at her age. She seemed outside of time.

Her smile lit up the room. "Thanks for letting me in. It must have been hard."

Lincoln thrust his hands into his pockets. This woman was enchanting, but he had so many questions. "You have to believe me. I tried everything to open the door but then it just did. There's a desk drawer I thought contained the key, but I didn't need it."

A light laugh escaped Alinta's shining lips. "Well, I did ask you to let me in. Maybe that was the key."

A revelation arrived and Lincoln snapped his fingers. He had seen her at the airport and now she was here, in the middle of nowhere. This strange place where he'd woken. If Outback Tours was behind this, surely she was part of the game. And if he was going to play along, she would be a beautiful woman to play along with. "Do you have something for me?"

Alinta arched an alluring eyebrow. "Whatever do you mean?"

A familiar flutter batted inside his gut. He needed to play the game first. "I guess you need me to ask the right questions."

She patted down the creases from her dress. "Who would lock you in here?"

Rusty hinges whined as he flicked down the seat of the chair and sat next to her. He couldn't blame Outback Tours. He'd opened the door to let her in, but she held the key to him getting back. "It had to be my friends."

Alinta smiled enticingly. Her sweet, enchanting voice

was like none Lincoln had ever heard before. "Some friends. Tell me about them."

"Well, the four of us graduated together fifteen years ago, and we decided to take this trip as a reunion of sorts. It's been great catching up with old friends."

Alinta studied him. "Has it?" As if sensing his discomfort she reached into her suitcase and withdrew a sandwich. "Would you like something to eat?"

Lincoln ripped away the plastic, the soft bread and tang of tomato heaven to his taste buds. This beautiful woman was playing her role well. He was sure she would give him the information he needed—the next step in this survival game he'd be thrust into—but a longer game could be played here. This wasn't about getting back to the campsite. If she was a bit player with Outback Tours, he could pick up this conversation around the campfire once they were all back. And, with a bit of luck, maybe the next part of his story included her.

Lincoln ran a hand through his grease-coated hair, hoping it was putting his best foot forward. "So what are you doing here?"

"I'm in a train station, and I'm in a waiting room. What do you think?"

"How did you get here?"

"I've already asked you that question, so I will answer yours after you answer mine."

Surely the flirtation wasn't part of the script required for this adventure game. The fluttering butterflies in his stomach landed, one-by-one on the excitement fizzing deep within him.

"I woke up here, and I presumed I'd been dropped off by—" He stopped. How much should he reveal that he knew she was part of the game? "The tour company. There, I've answered your question. Your turn."

Alinta cocked her head. "Okay. To answer your question, I was called out here. There is a job I was asked to do."

"What sort of job requires you to be out here?"

"I'm a guide." She lowered her eyes again before fixing him with a lingering look.

Lincoln smirked. *Of course you are.* He shifted on his creaking seat as he evaluated his internal playbook for his next move. He went for a tried-and-true home-run hitter. "So you're a guide. That's terrific. I'm a stockbroker—a pretty successful one, actually." He paused, allowing his success to land, and waited for the usual reaction. The telltale lift of an eyebrow, the slight parting of the lips.

Instead, Alinta yawned. "Really? Tell me your story."

I thought I had.

He leaned in toward her. "When I get back to the USA, I'll be snapping up that beach house at Half Moon Bay I've had my eye on and upgrading the car. You really need a convertible in Southern California."

A nervous smile replaced the yawn. Better.

The rest of his story poured out. His stellar rise in stock-broking, getting his toe on the lowest rung of the property ladder in San Francisco, and his swift climb. The awards for overachievement and the money. Hinted at in a perfected way.

She nodded, a polite smile for each achievement.

Lincoln hadn't felt this comfortable with a woman since . . . college. Dianne included. Lincoln's knee started to bounce, unable to contain the building excitement as the thrill of the chase ramped up. He ran out of career highlights and a silence descended.

Alinta arched an eyebrow at him, as an impenetrable façade dropped into place. "Well, that's what you do for a job, but your story is where you've come from, which has led to who you are."

A bell rang in the depths of his memory. He'd heard that before. Eddie, around the campfire. Lincoln's curiosity broke free of his restraint, driven by a need to prove he was smarter than she took him for. "You *are* from Outback Tours, aren't you?"

The leather creaked and cracked as Alinta shifted to face him. "No I'm not."

Lincoln furrowed his brow. "So who are you with?"

The ruby-red lacquer on her lips glinted with her simple, wordless smile.

Lincoln pressed on. "Well, if you aren't with Eddie, your competition is pretty bad. They set up this survival challenge

—or whatever it's called—and it was pretty poorly run. No warning, no preparation, nothing. They left me locked in here with no food and no way out."

"What makes you think I'm competition?"

"Well, what type of guide are you?"

"I think of myself more as a guide in life. I have a wealth of wisdom, and it's my duty to share that wisdom with those who follow."

"Like a relationship coach?"

"No, but I can help with that. I can help you be less 'unlucky' in love."

Lincoln narrowed his eyes. "What do you mean by that?"

"I can help you discover why your relationships always end the same way, with women walking away from you just when you think things are going well."

The fizzing and popping of the nerves in Lincoln's gut gave way to a familiar sinking feeling. He was being played.

"What do you think you know about my life?"

"More than you realize, but if you listen to what I have to say, you'll find your future won't have to stumble along the same rocky path of your past. And you might even avoid situations like receiving a letter demanding more than half of your possessions."

Lincoln breathed hard as he fumed. He knew who was behind this. "Eliza set this up, didn't she?"

Alinta's eyes softened. "No, she didn't set this up, but she certainly started it off."

TWENTY

The dying throes of the guttural humming bounced around the cave and landed softly on the smooth floor. In the half-light Bree pulled her hoodie tight as a waft of damp air forced a shiver out of her. Had she even heard the music? Or was her mind simply playing tricks to get her through this ordeal?

She pulled herself to her feet as her muscles screamed, her stomach aching for food. "Eddie?" She stood in a wide expanse of deep-red rock, lit by a tall sliver of light. The cave narrowed as it led to the light's source—a crack in the rock wall. A way out. It was thin, but she could squeeze through.

Her gaze followed the shaft of light as it cut through the dust now rising from the cave floor and spotlighted a rough wall daubed with lines and swirls of ancient art. Sloaney's words came back to her: *"Everyone goes too close and they lose the perspective."*

She backed away from the wall and the lines revealed

their meaning. The swirls became figures in white chalk and red ochre. People danced around a fire of charcoal lines. Bree recognized a kangaroo and a long, thin creature that had to be a snake. More unrecognizable shapes led to the largest of the figures daubed in yellow and white. Its arms spread wide, a hunter advancing on his prey. The wall was filled with story, preserved for the ages.

And she'd seen it before.

"Oh, how beautiful." Bree stepped farther back, and a dull clang sounded as a small terra-cotta bowl spun on the rock floor. It was full of tiny red berries and next to it, a small sign with neat, handwritten block letters: *Follow my example.*

Bree stared at the bowl. Her stomach made an overwhelming sales pitch to Eddie's warning that not all bush foods were fit for human consumption. And who left a sign like that? First, the didgeridoo, then food. She peered into the cave. "Eddie? Sloaney?"

In the silence questions whizzed around her head like outback flies. Once she escaped the cave she would need to find the campsite, and she needed the energy.

Her hunger wouldn't be denied. Bree picked up a small berry and stepped back into the shaft of light. As she gave the berry a squeeze, the skin cracked and juice dribbled down her finger. She lifted it to her nose and flicked her tongue at it. The sweetness exploded on her taste buds and she slipped the berry into her mouth and cautiously bit down. The warm juice had an edge of bitterness, but soon her mouth was filled by a rush of elation.

Her stomach roared its appreciation but demanded more. Bree stood waiting for the side effects, then picked up two more and chewed on them. The burst of sweetness flooded through her, and another handful went in, her senses tingling on overload.

Bree's eyes now adjusted to the dim light, and she moved toward the back of the cave, one tentative step after another. The floor changed to a gentle upward slope over smooth rocks polished by eons of flowing water before it flattened out, dust and feathers strewn across it. She shielded her eyes against the now-bright light pouring through the rip in the rock. A rip as wide as herself. Relief washed over her, chasing away the sugar rush of the berries.

She sensed the movement before she saw it. The slightest twitch at the foot of the rock, hidden in the shadows at the light's edges that led to her safety. A small bundle of dark-brown scales coiled underneath a reddish-brown head. A tongue lashing an evil smile.

Between her and freedom sat a snake.

———

The sun beat down on Eliza as she sat on her swag, trying to make sense of it all. She had been walking in a straight line for half a day. How could she arrive back where she started?

She pulled her water bottle from her backpack, pointlessly. The plastic crinkled as she returned it to her backpack. The answer wasn't clear, but the lesson was. They had sent her on a journey faced with choices and she had made the wrong ones. She was sure of it.

Bree. She had to get back for Bree. Her determination flooded back—all she had to do was return to the intersection and choose again. Left or right, she would make that decision when she got back there.

She looked again at the lowering sun. The swag had to come with her. Self-doubt made another pitch but she batted it away. She wouldn't need to be out here overnight. A tour company wouldn't allow that, would they?

Eliza unpegged the swag and knelt in front of it when she heard the low rumble. The cloudless sky was not the cause, but she was sure she'd heard that rumble before.

A vehicle. It had to be.

Maybe this swag was a checkpoint, and now that she'd found it, Eddie and Sloaney were on their way to pick her up. She'd learned her lesson and would take that home with her. Or maybe the lesson was deeper. When you found yourself in trouble, you needed to go back to the beginning and start again. She'd certainly been to enough self-help seminars to have heard that before. The beginning—that first trip to Africa fueled on adventurous spirit and bullheaded desire to make things right. So *that* was the lesson: she had to find that version of herself and reconnect.

Eliza shielded her eyes from the afternoon sun. The rumble grew as plumes of dust billowed from the road. She exhaled away her frustration as she savored her win. She had been on a harrowing, mind-bending trek through outback Australia and survived. On her own, with only herself to rely on.

Fueled by a fierce self-pride, she allowed her banished anger and indignation their moment. After the debrief—which always came at the end of these corporate personal development exercises—she would give them some honest customer feedback and a substantial piece of her mind.

The rumble quaked her calves as the shape emerged from the heat haze—a large box of a vehicle, red, not black, and significantly bigger than a four-wheel drive. It seemed to fill the entire width of the dusty track.

She reevaluated her options. Eddie had said there was little traffic out here, but she was in no position to argue with a stroke of fortune. A deadlier feeling pressed in on her. Lincoln said on the plane that the country was dangerous, and the threats extended beyond the creepy crawlies. The stories of people hitchhiking the back roads of Australia who were never heard from again.

Fear pulsed through her nervous system, setting her ablaze. While Lincoln could have talked up the danger, there was a chance in this he hadn't. Her empty water bottle lay in the red dirt alongside her only safe place in the outback.

What choice did she have? Her need for water and shelter outweighed whatever danger she might face.

The haze dissipated and the detail of the road train filled in, dust clouds flying alongside its long, thin body. Her overworked muscles shook—needing the rescue, dreading the threat. She had to get the driver's attention, regardless of the danger.

The danger of a random stranger was possible. The danger of dehydration or exposure was certain.

She jumped into the middle of the track, arms windmilling in the now-still, tinder-dry air. The rumble lowered into a deepening roar, and the giant vehicle slowed as it pulled to one side of the track. Eliza's heart thudded as she clenched her fists and twitched her calves, tensed for escape.

With a loud hissing and the squeal of brakes, the road train came to rest with a lurch, the red cabin and shining silver grill towering over her.

Red.

Through the windshield Eliza saw large sunglasses under a cap's visor. The cabin door flew open as every scenario between uncomfortable and catastrophic flashed before her eyes. She checked over both shoulders for somewhere to run.

The driver jumped to the ground, brushing hands on khaki shorts. Long, slender legs down to thick, chunky work boots. The driver removed the cap, and a rust-red ponytail swished from side to side.

The woman removed her sunglasses to reveal the most crystal-blue eyes Eliza had ever seen, sparkling above a crooked grin and grease-stained cheeks. "What are you doing out here, love? Not lost, are ya?"

Eliza fell to her knees, her chest heaving. But the tears wouldn't come. Not in front of a stranger.

TWENTY-ONE

The flat, brassy horns and chugging guitar drifted across the pub from the jukebox, along with an impassioned, croaking scream:

> *Out where the river broke*
> *The bloodwood and the desert oak*

Andy pushed aside the tiny plate, now filled with only a few pastry crumbs. "Do you have a car? How can we get back to the campsite?"

Smithy nodded along with Midnight Oil. "Where is the campsite?"

Embarrassed, Andy laced his fingers behind his head. He'd had no idea where the campsite was. "We are with Outback Tours. Two guys—Eddie and Sloaney. Do you know them?"

Smithy shook his head. "How did you end up here?"

Andy's conscience answered the question at a different level, and it didn't like the answer. "I walked. I woke up on a cliff above a river, which should be around here somewhere."

Smithy shrugged. "That could be anywhere out here."

Andy heaved a sigh, his pulse racing as an unwelcome option presented itself. He needed to stay off the grid and below the radar. "They've got a satellite phone. Could you call them for me?"

Smithy nodded at Andy's phone, facedown on the table. "Why can't you?"

"No coverage. So what can I do?"

Smithy took great care to place his glass back on its coaster. "We need to get you going where you need to be. Let's work it out. How long were you walking for?"

Andy's mental gears creaked into action. He woke at seven and it was now after two. His phone beeped and he shoved it across the table, unable to face the message.

Smithy frowned at him. "I thought you said you had no coverage."

How could he explain this? It would be hard enough to talk about being abandoned on a cliff top. It would be impossible to describe a disconnected phone that still received messages. And he couldn't talk about the deepest truth of all.

Another roar bellowed from the corner. Now a dozen people followed the parabolic path of the copper coins through the air.

Smithy put down his bite-sized pie and leaned toward Andy, a kindness in his eyes. "Is everything okay? You look a bit, I don't know the word for it . . . hunted?"

Andy's face warmed as his voice emerged in a staccato burst. "What makes you say that?"

"The way your gaze darts around the room, checking out everyone. Not wanting to use your phone. The only thing you look like you're interested in is the game of two-up."

"What's two-up?"

"An old gambling game that's been played since modern Australia began. Deceptively simple—all you need to do is bet on how two coins will land."

"Sounds likes it's pretty easy to get into."

"The best traps are."

Andy found another option with a snap of his fingers. The barman. "Back in a moment."

He pushed through the crowd and leaned on the bar as the tanned, sinewy young man in the red, yellow, and blue shirt downed the last of his beer. "Just in time, mate. Your shout?"

Shout? "I'm sorry, sir, I'll keep my voice down."

The young man clapped a hand on Andy's shoulder with a laugh. "Shout. It's Aussie for your turn to buy."

Andy shrugged off the hand whose grip was tightening. "I'm sorry, I've got no money."

The man's smile slid away at the rebuff, as from the

jukebox the brassy horns slid down the scale into silence, broken by more familiar finger-picking guitar. *"On a warm summer's evenin' . . ."*

The barman's meaty forearm landed on the bar. "It's okay, Tex, I've got this one." His expression hardened, his eyes like flint. "What can I do you for?"

Andy tried his broadest smile. "I was hoping to use your phone."

The barman jerked his head toward the door. "There's a pay phone out there. Takes coins." He reached for the cloth hanging over his shoulder and polished his way down the bar as he collected empty glasses.

Another dead end. Andy made his way back to the table, and Smithy drained his glass. "How did you do?"

"He's no help."

"Well, I can help you work out how to get you back on track."

The coins spun in the air again. Andy's little finger twitched as the coins clinked on the polished floorboards and rolled to a stop. All he had to do was guess how two coins would land, not pull off the point spread in the NBA Eastern Conference. How easy was that?

He reached for his drink, and Smithy's eyes clouded with a stern concern. "You've got a gambling problem, mate."

A statement, not a question. "How did you know?"

Smithy's head bobbed in a slow nod. "I've seen it before.

Can't take your eyes off it. Each time you look for a little bit longer, the corners of your mouth twitch. Gotta tell ya, it never ends well."

"It's only two coins."

Smithy cleared his throat and lowered his voice. "It's more than that. Much more. It's the rush, the temporary denial of consequences. It's the devil-may-care concern for the future to feed the uncontrollable desires of the present." The rough Australian in front of Andy appeared to have gone.

The doors to the kitchen swung open as the waitress hefted the largest deep-dish pizza Andy had ever seen. The waft of onion and tomato drifted in her wake, and Andy's mouth dropped open at the mound of meat and cheese now sitting on the table next to them. Andy implored Smithy. "Don't you have any more money?"

"Do you?"

"I've got to find a way . . ."

Smithy placed a hand on the table between them. "This is how it always starts, doesn't it?" His eyes hardened as they drilled into Andy's soul. "The desire rises and you justify how easy it is, how it won't be like last time. First with something small, then something larger. You dig to fill a small hole that your first gamble created, only to find that when it's full, you're standing in a larger hole. And that needs filling too."

Smithy's oddly poetic language belied a blunt, rough-and-tumble man still covered in the dust of the outback as he described every morning of Andy's year and his journey from college, starting with a first bet placed at Lincoln's insistence, whose insider news on the Flagstaff College basketball team made it a sure thing.

A wide crack ripped down the middle of Andy's resolve, and he could no longer hold back his story. Staggering through the outback while he lost hope. Waking on a cliff with no memory of getting there. Surviving an overnight dust storm. Enduring a campfire intervention by friends horrified at the depths to which he'd sunk. Lodging at the campsite in a crater in the middle of nowhere.

Smithy took it all in. "That's not all, is it?"

Andy dropped his head. "I thought I could disappear for a while. Get away from some big gambling debts." Guilt covered him like a heavy blanket. "Big ones."

"How big?"

Andy started to answer, then stopped. He swallowed hard and gave it a second run as he owned the size of the millstone around his neck. "In total? Seven hundred thousand dollars."

Tears formed in the corners of Smithy's eyes. "I'm so proud of you."

"Why?"

"You've been able to admit that to yourself."

Who was this guy? This dusty, solid water tank of a man had pried secrets from him in minutes and he somehow felt better for it. "Who are you?"

Smithy's voice was quiet. Soothing. Unthreatening. "I'm a guide. We all are."

"All?"

"Yes, all. We're here to help you on your journey."

"To get back to the campsite?"

"It's far more important than that."

Andy's stomach growled. Like a lion caged with its meal outside the bars. "If you want to help me on my way, I really need something to eat."

The waitress placed another pizza on the bar, and Andy's resolve deserted him. The steam rose to the shimmering heat flickering beyond the window. He couldn't venture back into the oven of outback Australia with no transport, no phone, and no idea of where he was headed. His hunger needed attention. "This is crazy. I should be able to talk the barman into helping a lost tourist."

Smithy shook his head. "That's not your biggest need."

Andy made his way back to the bar. The barman absent-mindedly picked at his fingernails with a corkscrew and raised an eyebrow. "Found some money, did you?"

Andy pushed aside the shame and nodded to the menu board with imploring eyes. "I'm a visitor to your country and I'm lost. My friend here is out of money—"

"Friend?"

Andy threw a glance back to the table. Smithy was gone. He would have to fix this on his own. "Look. I need something to eat, so maybe I could wash some dishes for you?" He lowered his head, hoping for mercy, expecting the inevitable crushing blow of rejection.

Andy looked up into the barman's nearly complete smile. "I tell you what, mate. You look like a bloke who likes a flutter, so how about you gamble for some lunch?"

TWENTY-TWO

This had to be a setup. The leather chair cracked as Lincoln retreated one seat back from Alinta. "What's going on?"

She offered him another shy smile but nothing else. "I can help."

"Help what? Get me back to the campsite?"

"No." She reached a hand toward him. "I can help you get out of the mess you've made of your life. Get back on track."

Lincoln shot to his feet as he scoffed at her. "The mess I've made of my life? Weren't you listening before? Once I get the convertible—"

"You'll drive yourself to an empty home." She padded away from him into the stationmaster's office.

Lincoln stormed after her, his eyes hunting for the hidden cameras he was certain were there. Probably being fed directly back to a truck his friends sat in, wicked smiles perched in front of the screen, enjoying his discomfort. This wasn't a competition. It was a setup.

"The others have to be behind this. There is no other way you would know details like that."

Alinta leaned back on the desk and crossed her feet. "I've never met your friends. Others have been chosen to provide them with guidance."

Lincoln closed his eyes in head-shaking exasperation. "What on earth are you talking about?"

"How did you get here, Lincoln?"

"How did I get here? I woke up in this strange building—"

"No. How did you get here at this moment in time, this juncture on the road of your life?"

Lincoln folded his arms to put a barrier between himself and this strange woman. "This juncture in my life?"

"Yes. How did you arrive here, with an impending divorce and the threat of losing it all? Where the disappointments of the past guarantee the roadblocks of your future?"

"What are you talking about?"

"I'm talking about your life, Lincoln. I'm talking about locking away the pain of your past but ensuring the un-happiness of your future. You locked yourself in here—"

His anger exploded. "How many times do I have to tell you that I didn't lock the door—"

Alinta quieted him with a raised hand. "What do you think I'm talking about?"

He was thrown. "This building, clearly."

"No." One word, pregnant with a weight of information.

"I'm talking about your life. Your unhappiness. The relationships that grind to a halt before they start. A marriage doomed before it began. Why do you think that is?"

Lincoln's indignation fought to the surface. "So I'm unlucky in love. Who isn't?"

"Maybe you hold the key to your unhappiness, but you don't realize it."

Keys? Unhappiness? He checked the timetables pinned to the wall to see when this woman's train was coming. "I don't buy any of this."

"So what do you buy? What explanation do you have for this?" Her voice hardened. Honey replaced by steel. "You wake up here with no sign of how you got here. One minute you're locked in, the next minute—after my request for you to let me in—you are free. What do you think is going on?"

Lincoln's anger ebbed, replaced by confusion. None of this made sense.

"I've seen this before—when someone locks in the past to protect themselves from danger or further pain. But it's what you lock out that causes you to run off the rails." She fixed her eyes on him. Strong but soft.

"Locking in the pain? This is a railway station . . ." His explanation petered out. "This has to be a hallucination." He thought back to the previous night. The bush food. That had to be it.

Alinta planted her hands on her hips. "So if I'm a figment

of your imagination, your conscience must know deep down what the problem is. So why don't you acknowledge it in case you're saved? *If* this is a hallucination. What have you got to lose?" Her eyes drifted to the desk.

"Are you saying whatever is in that desk drawer is something I put there?"

Alinta nodded. "Now you're getting it."

"That is insane. That drawer is locked tight."

"Like the door was."

Lincoln shook his head. "This is ridiculous. Let me show you how ridiculous it is." He stormed behind the desk, his fingers found the worn groove beneath the handle, and he maintained eye contact with Alinta in preparation of the point he was about to prove.

He jerked the drawer back, and as it flew open, his shoulder slammed into the wall. There was a gentle rattle as the drawer's contents bounced around. His brow furrowed as his mind raced. He took one look inside the drawer.

It wasn't a key.

He slammed the desk drawer shut but couldn't rationalize the mental picture now burned into him. In the desk drawer was a gift-ribboned box, one he'd planned to carry to the deserts of the Sahara to surprise the woman of his dreams.

And the box contained a ring.

The berries rolled across the cave floor and came to rest against the snake's pulsing scales. Its tongue tasted her direction and distance and entranced Bree with a silent, numbing fear. She crept backward, her eyes fixed on her would-be attacker. The first steps felt like quicksand, and her pace quickened with every step that put distance between her and a painful, slow death.

She leaned against the mouth of the cave, her head swimming as she looked skyward, at her only other avenue of escape. Another hundred feet of long slices in the rock, but the slight incline was no longer generous. The wall above her was vertical.

Her thumb throbbed, now coated with blood as her hands hung at her side. She shivered as the tears came. Frustration. Anger. Fear of failure, of consequences she could not face. Surely the others would come looking for her if she didn't reappear. But the fear didn't reach its high watermark like it usually did. She had overcome the crippling, swooning heights to reach the cave. She could do this.

Bree's stomach groaned again and she reached for another handful of berries before a thought stopped her hand cold. Bush food . . . Was the snake a hallucination? Maybe these berries had conjured up her greatest fear and placed it in the way of her escape. She spat them onto the cave floor and crept back to the fissure in the rock. The forked tongue sensed danger and the snake's head cocked back.

The words came slowly—the repetition building a case to convince herself this was a hallucination. *This is not real. This is not real. This is not real.*

The fear pulsing through her disagreed.

She lifted a foot to take another half step toward this figment of her imagination. The snake jerked as it lunged for her, and she screamed and jumped back. The snake's head struck a stone, which shot at her and hit her shin. A bolt of pain seared up her leg, and she rushed back to the mouth of the cave. She inspected her leg. Blood oozed from a stinging cut. The pain was very real.

This was no hallucination.

Bree cast a suspicious glance at the bowl of berries and the sign. *Follow my example.* Follow whose example? Was there something more in the wall painting? She peered at it. Kangaroos chased by small men wielding spears. The snake slithering away from the hunter. Should she follow his example? But he carried no weapon—he was drawn mid-stride, his arms out.

Fragments of memory dropped into place as she stared at the figure. This hunter reminded her of Eddie and how he'd moved on the snake, his hands wide, his voice flat.

Follow my example.

Eddie was behind this—he had to be—playing the music that had drawn her to the cave, the berries he'd harvested the day before. Just the idea of someone being near calmed her.

She'd already conquered fear once today, and she could do it again.

Bree made her way back to the rear of the cave, her nerves tingling. The snake eyed her from the safety of the shadows. Her heart rose to her throat as she held out quivering hands wide. She forced calmness into her tremoring voice as she ventured a cautious step toward the snake. "Careful now. Careful."

Vertical slits stared her down, evaluating if she was predator or prey.

Bree ventured another nervous step, her hands wide, her voice low. "Careful now. Careful."

Prey. With a sudden jerk, the snake lunged for her again.

TWENTY-THREE

S o where are you headed, love?"

Ice-cold water burned Eliza's throat as she guzzled from the bottle. The blasting air conditioner chilled her overheated skin to goose bumps. She couldn't keep up. One minute she was preparing to defend herself from a stranger on a baking, deserted dirt road; the next minute she was shivering in the front seat of a massive truck with a bright young woman called Grace. They flew above the outback—high above the road that had broken her—barreling along at a speed that seemed impossible ten minutes earlier.

Grace gripped the giant steering wheel, a deft touch guiding tons of metal as it powered through the approaching twilight. She flicked switches on the expansive dashboard, then flicked the chin of the stuffed wombat that sat on cracked leather, next to a bumper sticker that proudly asked and answered its own question: *How's my driving? I don't want to know.*

Grace veered around a trough in the road. "So how did you end up here?"

"I was participating in a journey of discovery—I believe they used to be called a walkabout."

"You did that on your own? Not very smart, I would've thought."

The CB radio's mic cord jiggled in Eliza's face as she absorbed the blows of Grace's disappointment. Even with a woman she didn't know, she never wanted to be thought of as any less than capable. "The tour group said they weren't going to do one, but they dropped me off next to this road. So I started walking . . ." She tried to corral the words into order, but they wouldn't cooperate. How could she talk about walking in straight lines and ending up where she started?

"If you tell me where you are headed, I can help you get where you need to go."

"Our campsite is in a crater next to a gravel track."

Grace grunted. "That could be anywhere out here. Any idea which direction you've come from?"

"Not really." On the truck's dashboard, one straight line sat alone on the GPS, like the flight path over the Pacific. "I guess you could take me back into town, and I could retrace our steps from there. But where did you come from?"

The cabin shuddered under more corrugation. "Like most of us, I came from where I started." She pointed to a sheaf of papers rubber banded to her sun visor. "This tells where I need to be." She reached across and tapped the GPS. "This gives me the right bearings. You've gotta have them to know you're heading the right way. Otherwise you'll get lost out here. You'll get lost anywhere."

That made profound sense, even if it came from a grease-smeared, ponytailed truck driver. "You sound like my life coach."

"You've got a guide already?"

"Tarquin's more someone who sits there while I talk."

"That sounds more like a dog than a coach." Grace bit her lip. "Tell me your story."

The stinging recollection of Eddie's rebuke shaped her response. "While I work in fashion . . ." She wracked her memory for something she did while not on the clock and came up empty. "I spend time . . ." Her thoughts deserted her and with a sigh she went back to her usual well. "I'm the second-in-charge at Virgo Fashion. We're a multinational company with a whole family of brands and ten thousand staff." She checked off her career achievements as if she were playing LinkedIn bingo. The highlights came easily, her tried-and-true script rolled out as if she were talking to the news, a fashion magazine, or her hand in a game of one-upmanship with an insecure man across their drinks on an ill-fated date.

A mob of twenty twitching kangaroos sat up at their approaching rumble before bounding away, and Grace leaned the road train away from them. "It sounds like you're doing some wonderful things, but you're a human being, not a human doing."

"I think I'm reaching the same conclusion. I've been asked to go for this job, which would be the pinnacle of my career, but I really don't want it. I know it's not a fear of failure, but . . ."

"Maybe you've been head down, charging ahead at some random point in the distance, and now that you're at that random point, you've looked up and thought, 'How did I get here?'"

Eliza chewed her lip as the outback scrolled past her window. This tour had turned into a mini version of her life—low flying through the outback at seventy miles an hour, with no idea of where she was, wondering where she was headed. And this young woman had pinpointed her restlessness in five minutes.

"Maybe you've been sucked into the trap of doing what's next and you've closed your eyes to what's needed."

In the distance another mob of kangaroos bounded across the road, but one stopped in the middle of the track and waited.

Grace winced. "This might not be pretty."

Eliza frowned. "Why? Can't you stop?"

The giant truck slowed, the gears screaming as Grace worked down through them. "Most truckies out here wouldn't risk their cargo by swerving, so they would simply go over it."

Eliza saw the reason for the kangaroo's pause. A tiny figure, a joey, slowly hopped across the dirt track toward its mother. "We have to stop. Slow down."

Grace geared down again, the engine shrieking at its overwork.

Eliza slammed a hand on the dashboard. "Stop, Grace!" Her heart pounded in her ears as her scream filled the cabin. *"Stop the truck!"*

Grace threw everything onto the brakes. An unholy squeal pinched Eliza's ears as the cabin filled with the acrid scent of burning rubber. "Hold on."

Eliza closed her eyes as the truck jerked to a stop, wrenching her from her seat. She opened one eye, then the other, and stood to see the kangaroo five feet from them. Its ears twitched, and a tiny head poked out from its midriff.

Eliza jumped from the cabin. The reason for the kangaroo's reticence wasn't only the joey. A large cut on its leg oozed a deep red.

"It's okay." She slowly approached the animal, who turned and limped its way from the track, a painful hop taking it into the bush. Eliza wiped a tear from her eye as she climbed back into the truck. She'd saved two kangaroos and she couldn't wait to tell Bree.

Grace was silent as the truck resumed its speed.

"I can't believe truck drivers just run over the top of such beautiful creatures—especially ones with babies."

Grace geared up again. "You get really wound up when you really care about something, don't you?"

"What do you mean?"

"I get the sense that it's been a while since you've felt that happen."

Eliza snapped a look at her. "What are you talking about?"

"It makes a difference to you when you do the right thing rather than sticking to the schedule. It's nice to see."

That sounded surprisingly New Age for a female Australian trucker pushing a giant truck through the dusty outback. "So where are we exactly?"

Grace nodded to the glove compartment. "Why don't you go old school? If you look at the map in there, you might see something familiar. It might help."

Eliza snapped open the latch and reached for a neatly folded map. The sheet of paper grew with each unfold until it covered her half of the cabin. The map was dominated by a single thick line that ran down its middle, intersecting with a smaller road right in the center. Small tracks branched off from this major road. At the bottom of the map, closely drawn contours hugged tight around a hill labeled *Flagstaff*.

"Hey, that's the name of my college."

A smile crept across Grace's face. "Anything there you recognize?"

Eliza scanned the terrain on paper. "Nothing. I presume this road in the middle is a highway or an interstate?"

"Have another look."

Nothing was recognizable or even stirred a memory. She let her eyes drift to the top of the vibrating sheet of paper. A black-and-white rectangle marked the map's scale, and beneath it was a compass designating the four directions for orientation.

Eliza's breath deserted her and her heart stopped beating. "What is this?"

Grace checked the rearview mirror as she eased off the accelerator. "What do you think it is?"

Eliza's eyes were drawn to the compass. In between the elegant calligraphy of the *N* and the *S* and nestled neatly between the flourishes of the *E* and the *W* was a face.

Her own.

TWENTY-FOUR

The heat drained from Lincoln's face as his shaking fingers found the wall. No one knew about that box. No one. He wanted Eliza to be the first to know about it, and he had been too proud to own up after the crushing rejection. His voice eked out in a thin whisper. "Who are you?"

"I told you, I'm a guide." She nodded to the desk. "What's in there?"

"How did it get in there?" He wrenched at the drawer again, but it was stuck fast.

Alinta stepped closer. "How did what get in there?"

Lincoln furiously massaged his temples. "This isn't real. You aren't real."

"I am. We all are."

"All?"

"Yes, we were all called on to help each of you discover how you got to this point in life and which road you will take from here. Not back to the campsite, but in life."

Each of us? What had happened to the others?

"So what's in there?"

Lincoln tried to force some sense into the situation, and the answer that slipped out made no sense. "Something from college. But how—?"

Alinta perched on the desk's edge. "By locking away the hurt, you've locked out so much more." Compassion radiated in her deep smile and seemed to emanate from her eyes, almost like love. "Tell me what happened in college."

Lincoln slumped to the floor and sighed as the memory he'd long confined wriggled free. "I was ready to move things to the next level, surprise her on the plains of Africa, but she decided an entry-level job in fashion was more important." He flushed as the bitterness of his past washed back to the shore of his present. "She told me if things were meant to be, she would pick things up when I got back. But when I did, she didn't."

Alinta's eyes softened. "I'm so sorry. That must have hurt."

Lincoln's words didn't make an appearance, but Eliza's face did. It flitted across his memory, but not one lit by the flames of the campfire or forty thousand feet above the Pacific in business class. Her face was younger, fresher, tauter—and sitting under a mortarboard.

Steel returned to his voice. "Yeah, but I moved on."

"Really?"

"Yep, put the whole thing behind me. There are plenty more fish in the ocean, so I went fishing."

"And how did that work out for you?"

"Even after I thought things were going well, there was always a point where the women left. I was unlucky, I guess." He scoffed. "And then I made the mistake of getting married."

"Do you know what's common to all those relationships?"

Lincoln raised an eyebrow. "What? That I haven't found the right person yet?"

"No. The common ground here is you."

Lincoln rose from the floor, his breath shallow, a deep ache settling into his clenched jaw. "So you're saying all this is my fault?"

Alinta shook her head. "Those relationships that never went anywhere . . . do they follow the same pattern?"

Faces circled through his mind—a carousel of women he had pursued. Their stories followed the same script. The thrill of the chase. Dangling his wealth like a baited hook. The announcement of togetherness made in the right places. But then the ring of words that became hollow and angry, echoing through the years. Closed off. Shut out. Weighing the right way to talk of the inevitable separation. And the reflection with an unanswerable question: *What have I done wrong?*

Lincoln lowered his head. The answer was always that he should know, but it left him with nothing but emptiness.

Alinta reached for his shoulder. "I've seen this before. By locking yourself away, you've almost guaranteed that you will be rejected."

Lincoln shook off her hand, but the anger within him met a ceiling. A barrier to his indignation. A recognition. A hint of truth to what she was saying.

"The rejection must have been crushing, but carrying it continues to hurt you. Crack the shell around you and be the man you were made to be."

Alinta again reached for his shoulder. "If you don't deal with this, you are just guaranteeing pain in the future. You will continue to shut out those you claim to love."

This time Lincoln didn't shake her off. The line from Dianne's letter. "What did you say?"

Tears welled in Alinta's eyes. "You've blocked out so much and so many because you've been shaped by pain."

"Shaped by pain?" Lincoln's pulse thudded in his ears as his indignation smashed through her insight. "I am totally in charge of what happens in my life."

Alinta smiled softly through the tears. "How's that working out for you? Even if you don't lose much because of that letter, it will keep happening until you actually acknowledge what is causing it. If you want to change your path, which started from the wrong point, you need to address that."

Something about this woman stopped his usual defensive posturing. It wasn't her beauty or even the strangeness of long-locked-away memories appearing in front of him in a locked desk, in a locked office, in the middle of nowhere.

It was the fact she was right.

The trader in Lincoln awoke. In every deal there was always a catch. He'd buried enough over the years to know that. "So what's the price?"

Alinta laughed. "You still don't get it, do you? This isn't a transaction. It's my job to bring it to your attention and guide you. I can't fix it, but I can give you tools to help you deal with whatever comes next."

Lincoln nodded. "So what do I do?"

"Let me see what's in that drawer."

Lincoln stared at the desk drawer, then back at Alinta. Doors that didn't open, then did. Drawers that held memories long locked away.

This is crazy.

He stormed outside and the heat assaulted him. He swept away the flies as the sun inched lower and the blue of the sky surrendered to a dusky pink, dusting the shimmering landscape with pastel hues to chase away the harsh reds and oranges. The only red that stood before him came from the railway signal watching over him, unblinking, and the buffer stop blocking the line was still in place.

Lincoln weighed his options. If he were to leave, he'd be heading out into the middle of nowhere with no idea of his direction. Alinta was his only hope. He trudged back inside.

She leaned against the desk, ankles crossed, the lowering sunset peering over his shoulder and catching the gold flecks in her raven hair. And the honey in her voice was back.

"I'm glad you've made that choice. When people can't answer my question of who they are, it's because they hide behind the facade of who they want people to think they are or what they promise they'll end up becoming. Not who they are now, or how they got there."

Lincoln absorbed her truth like a boxer on the ropes.

"I can read your face like a book, your heart even more so. When you talk of Eliza, it carries a depth of emotion as if she wounded your soul."

The first of the evening chill crept into the room. He might have spent a life fishing, but Eliza was the one who got away.

Alinta traced the timetables with a finger. "The last time this line was open, you were graduating. And the last time this door was opened, you were closing the door to your heart. So please, will you let me in and share what hurt you?"

TWENTY-FIVE

E liza's bouncing face stared back at her from the center of the compass. "What is this?"

Grace gripped the steering wheel as more corrugation rattled Eliza's teeth. "It might explain why you're feeling lost."

They raced past a sprawling gum tree beside the road and a leaning wooden sign gesturing down a dirt track no wider than a bicycle. Grace pointed it out. "I'll bet that leads somewhere exciting."

Eliza dropped her attention to the map. Her photo surveyed a journey that was featureless. Anything but exciting.

Grace leaned across to her, the setting sun sparkling in her sunglasses. "You won't find that road on your map."

Eliza limply shook her head.

"The road on that map looks like it's only going one way. I get that. I'm head down, barreling along the road most of the time.

"When I get the orders for my next drive, I rely on those above me to give me directions."

Eliza scoffed. "If you are making some kind of veiled reference that I need help from anyone else—"

"It's not veiled, and it's about now that people usually ask—"

The question burst from Eliza's lips. "Who are you?"

Grace tugged her cap's visor. "And there it is! I'm a guide, and it's my job to give you the perspective you can't get from inside your own life."

"So you're not a truck driver?"

Grace cocked her head. "What do you think? I appear out of nowhere, at the precise moment you're about to give up? In my glove compartment is a map with your face on it." She smiled. "It's about now that people start telling me this isn't real, but it is. Let me tell you about the people I've had in my cabin who've told me that. They all claimed they were fine being at the center of their life, but none of them were happy. Successful, maybe. Overachieving, maybe. Fulfilled? Rarely."

Another mob of kangaroos bounded into the bush. "So you're not taking me back to the campsite?"

"We'll get there; we need to take our time."

Eliza tensed as Lincoln's story again flared to life.

Grace playfully slapped at Eliza's leg. "You don't need to worry about anything. Tell me, how did you get here?"

"I've already told you I don't know how they got me from the campsite."

There was a kindness in Grace's eyes. "You know I don't mean only the campsite. How did you get here in life?"

"I don't know, mostly working hard. Taking the opportunities in front of me. Getting ahead."

"Getting ahead of what?"

The question was one she'd never had the insight to ask, or the courage to consider.

"Whenever I've asked people what they're getting ahead of, few of them know."

The reason for Eliza's disillusionment unveiled itself. She had planned everything in her career up until this point but had not once stopped to check what was driving her. Or who.

"There's something missing, isn't there?"

Eliza's cheeks burned in the frosty air. *That* conversation again. "If you're talking about having a man in my life—"

"I'm not saying that at all. The thing that's missing is a sense of something beyond yourself." Grace nodded at the map bouncing on Eliza's lap. "I think the map is telling you why. Your decisions seem to start from that reference point, so maybe for the next part of your journey it might be worth asking if that's the best place to be starting from."

Eliza sunk into the sheep's wool. The spongy wool on her seat back tickled Eliza's ears, as the lesson unfolded in her hands.

She had a decision to make but no idea how to make it.

Grace eased off the accelerator. "It's okay. You live in a world that only values you if you achieve, even more so if you overachieve. It ranks you by what you do over who you are and trains you that you can only trust yourself. How has that gone for you?"

The truck powered toward the sun that sagged in the afternoon sky. Eliza's decisions were based around what was best for her, despite how she'd dressed it up as everything but. "I can't change overnight."

Grace nodded. "Who can? Cast your mind back. What's the one decision that haunts you, that makes you wonder about the road not taken?"

Eliza's mind didn't have to travel far. The invitation from Virgo Fashion had come later than she'd hoped. Two weeks before their trip to Africa, which was a roadblock to the opportunity of a lifetime. The right thing to do at the time. The disconnection with Lincoln had occurred while he was away, before a world of shared experience through social media confirmed Bree's concerns.

And the certainty of a good career had outweighed the nebulous nature of a relationship that was moving a little fast for her anyway. But she had been forced into stamping down the green shoots of doubt that sprung up in drier times. She had made the right decision, but doubt had stoked the wondering.

"It was the right thing for my career."

More corrugation rattled Eliza to the core and Grace's silence was loud.

"So that's how you got here. But where is here?"

More dry, dusty, barren land flashed past Eliza's window.

"That decision started you on a path to this moment in time. I'm not saying that decision is wrong, but you're certainly in this place because that was the direction you faced when you started out."

"So you're saying if I married someone, then I'd be happy?" Eliza clenched her fists in her lap.

"I'm not saying that at all. Do you remember that path back there? That could lead somewhere exciting, but we'll never know because we're not even aware of the possibilities it could bring."

The reason for Eliza's discomfort in her near future. Possibilities. As she'd arrived at this point in life, her options had narrowed and narrowed as she'd plowed through her career. And the possibilities of her youth—when the world was her oyster—were all but gone.

"Eliza, as you arrive at the crossroads of your life, maybe you need to address a bigger issue. One that speaks to who is the reference point and the size of the choice you're about to make."

In Eliza's hands the map shuddered, and in its center, alongside the thick line of Eliza's life, three words appeared, one after another.

CEO.

Virgo.

Fashion.

The words shimmered as they solidified.

Grace turned kind eyes toward her and smiled. "You're about to face the biggest decision of your life, so perhaps the best time to revisit that is now."

TWENTY-SIX

Andy took a deep breath as he calculated the odds. The barman folded his arms, a gap-toothed grin creasing his face, and nodded at the pizza on the bar. "How about we start here? I'll give you one for free. Get it right and you can have a slice of my dinner."

"Free?"

"What are you waiting for?"

A risk without consequences. The music died away as a hush settled on the crowd.

"All right."

"No!" Smithy screamed as he emerged from a doorway and thrust his way through a crowd that closed around him, blocking his path. "You don't need to do this."

The barman's whisper slithered over Andy's shoulder, carried by a hint of mint and cigarette smoke. "What have you got to lose?"

Smithy shouted above the throng, as the crowd jostled him. "To start the next part of your journey, you need to leave this part of your journey behind. Take a stand. This weakness will continue to sabotage you unless you deal with it now."

"Sabotage?" The whisper caressed his ears. "We're talking about onions and bacon, cheese and mushrooms."

Andy's decision was locked in as the sweet steam rose from the pizza. He gave a slow nod. A tear left a wet, meandering trail down Smithy's dusty cheek as he stopped fighting against the crowd.

A huge cheer filled the pub as Andy made his way to the game of two-up. The man in the wide brown hat stepped forward and handed a wooden paddle to Andy. His fingers wrapped around the cold wood of the handle as the itch buried deep within him flared to life.

The man placed a thick hand on Andy's shoulder. "All you need to do is call—two heads, two tails, or a head and a tail. Then flip. How easy can it be?"

Andy's gambling instinct calculated the best odds. "One head and one tail."

"Come in spinner!" the man roared to the crowd.

Andy flung the pennies into the air and they spun, catching the setting sunlight. The first coin landed with a crack on the wooden floor and rolled to a stop.

"It's a tail."

The second coin seemed to slow before it hit the floor with a sharp crack. It spun, and spun, and came to rest.

"And a head."

Andy exhaled in sheer relief at the victory as he made his way back to the barman. He gave a sneering thumbs-up to Smithy, who simply shook his head, his eyes downcast.

The barman pushed the pizza pan closer to Andy. "There you go, mate, you've earned it."

With trembling fingers Andy lifted out a slice. Long strings of delicious cheese stretched as he raised the slice to his mouth, his senses in overload. As his lips clamped down on the first bite, tangy tomato stung his lips and satisfaction coursed through him. This was possibly the best slice of pie he'd ever had.

"One little gamble and look at this." Andy lifted the half-eaten pizza slice to Smithy in triumph.

The whisper at his shoulder was back as a meaty hand landed on his back. "Would you like to go for the whole thing?"

The crowd sucked in its collective breath, their entire focus on Andy as they edged forward. Hard, sweating faces pasted with fresh sneers that crinkled noses and narrowed eyes.

Andy flicked his gaze between the pizza and the coins, the coins and the pizza. He shoved the last of the crust into his mouth and crunched down on it. But it left him only partly satisfied.

Smithy wriggled through the crowd and placed a hand

on Andy's arm. "This is an important crossroad for you. In order to continue on life's journey, you need to say no. Put old choices behind you."

Andy's stomach growled again and drowned out Smithy. "I'll be fine." He headed back to the man in the hat, and the barman roared, along with an outback pub full of revelers. "Come in spinner!"

A surge of adrenaline jolted through Andy as the gambler within him stayed with the best odds. "One head, one tail." The coins spun and spun through the air. The first coin plummeted to earth and hit the floorboards with a slam.

"It's a head."

The second coin arced back to the floorboards, hit them with a clunk, and rolled on one edge. Rolling, rolling, in an ever-tightening circle in front of Andy. It came to rest. The man in the wide brown hat leaned over it, and Andy was overcome with a heady mix of alcohol and smoky ashes. "Another head."

Andy turned back to the barman and threw a disheartened look at the pizza. *Oh well.* At least he'd had something. He froze at the barman's manic stare—his eyes unblinking, a sneer pasted on a face now bereft of a smile, broken or otherwise.

Andy forced a smile to combat this searching, unfriendly shift. "I guess I'd better go and wash some dishes for you. Point me to the kitchen."

An angry, rumbling silence descended on the pub. Every face now scowled at him.

The barman folded his arms. "I'm not sure you realize how this works. You now owe more than that."

———

Bree screamed as the snake landed short of her. She kicked out as she scrambled back to the safety of the mouth of the cave. The blood that had pounded through her ears dropped to her feet as if looking for somewhere to hide.

What was she doing wrong?

She looked again at the sign: *Follow my example.* She did! It didn't work. The figure on the cave wall chased away the snake, its arms wide. She closed her eyes to summon back the memory. Eddie crouching low on the path, his arms wide, his voice flat. Her eyes snapped open as one minor detail filled in, completing the puzzle.

Eddie had been tapping his foot in a steady rhythm like tapping sticks.

With one eye on the snake, Bree stepped closer to the painting. The hunter chasing the snake had his arms wide, but one foot was higher than the other. Bree breathed in courage and as she steeled herself, calmness settled on her. For as long as she could remember, fear had bullied her into accepting herself as a failure. But fear had been conquered on the ravine wall, and she was armed with the secret of someone who had been a success.

Now fueled by the confidence of following a path taken, she put her arms out wide, the quiver now gone. She crouched and slowly made her way toward the snake. "Careful now. Careful."

The snake tasted the air.

Bree tried to tap her foot. At first her toes barely touched the ground, but they found it and developed a rhythm, a beat for her escape.

The snake lifted its head at the vibration, swaying left and right in time with the up and down of her foot. The vertical slashes lost their glare and seemed to gloss over. Mesmerized. Bree took another shuffling step forward, her tapping foot settling into its rhythm. "Careful now. Careful."

She stepped to the side as the snake leaned away from her as if checking the mouth of the cave. And it started a slow slither toward it.

Bree's confidence rose higher as she fought to keep time with her toes. She fought the urge to rush to the crack in the rock as the path to the exit cleared.

The snake slithered down the floor's incline and wrapped itself around the ceramic bowl. Bree's breath came in ragged gasps as she surveyed the gap in the rock. The heat from beyond her rock prison pulsed through to her—it had to be the way out. She could make her way through sideways.

She sucked in more breaths for courage and edged her way into the gap, the claustrophobia pressing in as the roughness of the rock brushed the back of her head. Her hot breath bounced back at her from inches away. She faced the warm breeze and edged her way through the gap as the walls narrowed.

The gap veered around a bend, and Bree navigated a jutting finger of rock that scraped her hips. She could see outside—the ruled line between blue sky and red sand.

Her adrenaline raced along with her breathing as the rock narrowed and pinched at her. Ten steps, maybe twelve. The rock narrowed further. This time it didn't pinch—it grabbed at her hips in an unmoving pincer grip, and she became a still life of desperation, pinned mere feet from freedom.

Fear oozed back.

She was stuck.

TWENTY-SEVEN

With a single nod Lincoln unlocked a world of hurt he had kept under lock and key for more than half his life.

Tears rolled down Alinta's cheeks as she stepped up to the desk and rested her hand in the wooden groove below the handle. With a short, sharp breath she tugged at the drawer and it responded to her touch.

Alinta's hand flew to her mouth. "I'm so sorry." She reached in and withdrew the tiny black box, its white ribbon still tied tight. "She didn't reject you in the moment. She rejected you for the future as well."

Her insight landed on him hard, and what rose in him wasn't the usual defiance or fury. Lincoln stared at the box in her hands—a box he'd sworn would never again see the light of day—and in anger's place was a sad vulnerability.

Alinta's finger flicked at the ribbon. "I can see why you wanted so desperately to lock it away."

Lincoln simply nodded as words failed him.

"You can entrust it to me."

The vulnerability that had numbed his limbs ebbed away.

Alinta placed the box on the edge of the desk and frowned into the drawer. "There is something else in here."

Lincoln rushed around to the drawer, uncertain of what to expect.

Alinta pulled out a circle of twine, red-and-black string woven into a bracelet.

Lincoln's mouth dropped open and stayed there. He'd last seen the gift from the children of the African orphanage the day after Eliza's polite refusal of his invitation for coffee, when every memory of his time on the dark continent had been shoved into a box for disposal.

"You were locking away more than rejection."

"What, an old bracelet made by kids?"

"No, a symbol of your care for others, from a time when the happiness of others meant as much to you as your own."

Alinta slipped it over his wrist with a simple nod. The light touch on his skin brought back memories of the first time he'd worn it—fresh from the biting disappointment in Eliza not coming with him, swirling with the pride in seeing the gratitude of beaming schoolchildren sitting in the new classroom he'd helped build. It felt like another Lincoln altogether.

He accepted Alinta's offered hand, her smooth skin soft

and warm. Beyond the door, a gentle wind whipped across the platform.

"Lincoln, it's been my pleasure."

"Where are you going?"

"My job here is done. I'm needed elsewhere."

The gentle howl picked up as the wind grew and blew dust through the open door.

"Where? Nothing's out there."

"There's a whole world out there. Maybe you should think about letting it in. You'll be far better off if you do. Far less unlucky." She slipped her silken hand out of his grasp and turned to the door. Behind her, dust whipped along the platform as the sunset illuminated her from behind, the golden flecks in her raven hair glowing as they were tousled by the growing wind.

Lincoln took a step forward, his hand still warm from her touch. "But what about my ex-wife's letter wanting a divorce?"

"I've given you the tools you need, Lincoln. Perhaps viewing your 'stuff' as objects and not the reason you are attractive would be a good start."

"But how am I going to get back to the campsite?"

Alinta smiled. "Trust me, you'll make it." She stepped through the door into the sandstorm.

Lincoln stood fingering the African bracelet as Alinta's life lessons took root. On the desk sat the tiny gift box, wrapped in its white ribbon. Alinta had forgotten it. He snatched it up and raced for the door.

"Alinta!" He shielded his eyes against the flying dust and howling wind and then, as if someone had flicked a switch, the wind was gone.

———

The words in the center of the map stared back at Eliza. Grace was right. Maybe subconsciously this was why she had balked at the CEO decision, even from the moment the chairman had suggested it. She wasn't fulfilled, and each decision was pushing her away from ever finding it.

Grace geared down as two emus flashed across the dirt road and disappeared into the fading light. "It's hard being at the wheel of your own life when you're driven every day. I won't go as far as accusing you of pride because it often generates a defense that pride is somehow a virtue. But who will be your reference point, Eliza?"

Eliza shifted to analysis—a safe default mode populated with facts to stave off emotion and vulnerability. And she landed on the default position she always found. "I can't trust anyone else."

"Why do you think that is?"

Eliza didn't have an answer, just the overwhelming sense of responsibility, tinged with something bitter. Something that had been part of her for a long time. "I've always had to rely on myself."

"This is about pride and feeling that your perspective is the only one that can be trusted. But if that perspective is what led you here and you're unfulfilled, something has to change."

Grace eased off the speed. "Being at the center of your life will almost certainly leave you unfulfilled."

Eliza scoffed. "So you're saying I should help others? Finally make the trip to Africa and dig wells or hug orphans?"

Grace winced and Eliza blushed, surprised at the depth of emotion that had exploded in response to a simple question.

"It's far deeper than that. It's choosing a different reference point. One that's bigger than you. One that's longer lasting than you. One that allows you to explore these side journeys that might bring your fulfilment. Or fun. Or—and this is the important one—making a difference in your world in the time you've been given. Maybe you only need to see the difference. If you do want to stay with yourself in control . . ."

The paper again shuddered and the words in front of her pulsed on the page. *CEO. Virgo. Fashion.* They thickened as all other lines on the map disappeared except one. The thick line right up its middle.

Grace waved her hand. "There are other alternatives." The three words again shimmered but this time evaporated.

The face on the compass faded away as the map sprung to life. Branches jutted from the solid line of the main road. Forks painted into her journey that led to short tracks and long highways. Intersections and roads less traveled. Eliza's finger traced them as they filled in, and the map became an elegant masterpiece of options.

"What are these roads?"

"I don't know. It depends on whose face appears as your reference point."

"It's a big decision, isn't it?"

Grace nodded. "For some people it's the biggest. Taking themselves out of the driver's seat and placing someone else at the wheel. I didn't say it was easy, but the best decisions rarely are."

Eliza stared at the chaotic riot of new lines now covering the map. She wondered, along with her wandering fingers, where these roads could take her. What she could see. Who she could become. She wondered where these roads led and, for the first time in a long time, that wonder came without fear. Fear that was deeper than making the right decision, but instead fear of making the wrong one. Fear of being seen heading in the right direction rather than knowing she was doing it. But with that fear came excitement, not nerves but genuine anticipation.

She nodded. "Okay."

The glowing thumbprint in the sky kissed the horizon

and caught the glint of the tears that rolled down Grace's cheeks. "I know I've said pride can be a bad thing, but I'm so proud of you."

Tears stung Eliza's eyes as the pressure of the past five years—even longer—was released. And with the relief came a sense of exhaustion—not from five hours hiking in the outback, but from life. Plowing ahead, head down. Ticking off one box after another. "So what do I do? How do I know who to use as my reference point?"

"The eternal question." She tapped the work schedule rubber banded to her sun visor. "As for me, I trust those above me."

The road train shuddered as Grace worked her way down through the gears. "You might find it hard to believe, but once you hand over control, you can still end up at the right place. Look."

Eliza followed Grace's pointed finger out the windscreen and down the road. In the fading light the truck's light flashed yellow as they caught a sign. A crossroads, like one she had confronted before this encounter with this strange, kind, young woman driving several tons of metal. A ticking filled the cabin, as Grace snapped her turn signal into service. The engine roared and lurched as she geared down.

"Someone else is in the driver's seat, and that's okay. You still made it."

TWENTY-EIGHT

A desperate claustrophobia clawed at Andy as the angry, murmuring crowd moved in with menace. A wave of jostling sweat washed over him.

The barman's face carried a sneering grin. "Sounds like the story of your life, mate. Looks like you've got a debt, and I like to collect on my debts."

Andy's eyes surveyed the pub for an escape. The door behind the crowd buzzed with activity as flies zigzagged behind the dirty screen. "I'll be happy to work here for the day or the week."

The crowd edged closer, their animosity boxing him in. Folded arms over checked shirts, narrow-eyed glares, and twitching sneers.

Andy's desperation poured out of him. "I can do anything for you—"

The barman slapped his hand on the counter. "I'm not interested in you working for me, Yank. I am only interested in collecting what is owed to me."

Andy's breath quickened. "But you never outlined what the consequences would be."

"I think you knew, Andy. You always do."

"Once I get back to the campsite, I'll be able to get my credit cards—"

Smithy stepped forward, shoulder to shoulder with Andy. "I would be willing to pay his debt so we can get on with getting him back on track."

The barman rolled his eyes. "How many times are you going to offer to do that?"

"As many times as I need to."

Andy snapped a look at Smithy. How many times?

The barman jerked his head toward Andy. "Well, as always, it's his call."

The familiar noose of impending failure tightened around Andy's neck. He was trapped, and he was going to end up owing someone. Again.

Smithy turned to Andy, a kindness in his eyes. "I am prepared to pay your debt. In fact, that's all I've got left."

"But you only had twenty dollars left—"

The barman dropped his meaty forearm on the bar, a sneer framing his gap-toothed grin. "You'll end up owing him and you've got no idea what he'll do with you."

Andy's finger twitched as the crowd edged in, pushing him back against the cold wooden lip of the bar.

Smithy placed a hand on Andy's shoulder. "Please?"

The barman leaned harder on the bar, his words carried by a hint of mint and cigarette smoke. "I tell you what, Andy. How about I offer you double or nothing? Take your chances, like you always do. Your luck has to change, doesn't it?"

Smithy placed a hand next to the barman's arm, his smooth complexion showing up the publican's red, blotchy skin. "This choice is not just about now. This can all end, if you allow me to take care of this for you."

Another heavenly waft of tomato and onions drifted from the kitchen and the barman sniggered. "How about I throw in a free pizza for having a go?"

The last straw of Andy's resistance broke in the same way it always did. He kicked the can of responsibility a little farther down life's road and nodded at the barman. He snapped his fingers as a cheer rose from the crowd. Smithy fixed his eyes on Andy, eyes clouded with concern. "I won't be far away."

The man in the brown hat stepped through the crowd, offering a wooden paddle to Andy. He gripped it with trembling hands. The coins wobbled as they were placed on the wood and Brown Hat leaned into Andy as he delivered his usual words. But the excited shout was gone; instead the words oozed out with a menacing whisper. "Come in spinner!"

"Come. In. Spinner. Come. In. Spinner." The crowd chanted with the man in the brown hat, their voices rising as Andy stared at the pennies on the paddle. One head, one tail.

He had to play the odds, but the gambler in him reminded him he'd already been burned. He had to try something different. He looked up to ask Smithy for advice, but the space where he had once stood had been absorbed by the chanting crowd. He surveyed the faces around him. Manic stares and chanting lips. "Come. In. Spinner."

"Two tails." Andy flung them into the air as the crowd roared. The pennies spun and arced in the air, glinting in the lowering sun that streamed through the pub's windows. They fell back to earth as the crowd fell back, and the pennies landed together, on their faces, with a sharp crack.

Andy leaned over them, one eye closed against possible bad news. One head. He staggered back against the bar. The other penny landed, its fate irrelevant.

A rumbling riffled across the crowd as they stepped forward. Andy frantically scanned them for Smithy, his only friend. The now-grinning barman wiped his hands on the tea towel hanging over his shoulder and lifted the counter to walk out from behind the bar.

The panic in Andy reached the lip of his resolve and spilled over. With one final glance at the faces in the crowd surrounding him, he did what he'd always done.

He ran.

Andy pushed through the crowd and threw open the pub's screen door, which slammed shut behind him as the heat assaulted him in a wave. The rise to his right. Open plain to his left. The Outback Tours four-wheel drive had headed in that direction. He would have to keep going down that road until he found them. Or Smithy.

Andy stumbled off the verandah, his shoes squeaking in the dirt. And he ran, expecting a pub full of patrons to follow.

———

The glowing thumbprint in the sky blinked as Bree closed her eyes. Whoever had placed those berries had made it out, so she could as well. Bree had already kicked fear to the curb twice, and it no longer reached even halfway to its old high watermark.

Six feet to sunlight. She breathed deep, control flooding back and washing away the panic as she evaluated her options. While the rock walls were too tight for her hips, there was another way to do this. Bree took a half step back toward the cave and lowered her body two inches. The pincer grip of rock now reached for the soft flesh of her belly rather than the hard bone of her hip. She breathed as the rock kneaded her flesh and stood tall as the gap in the rock opened out.

Her ankles turned on pebbles as she stepped into a small chasm of rock ten feet high: a mini version of the ravine. But unlike the ravine she had escaped, this one was open. A gust of wind blew dust and swirling debris past the entrance. Bree covered her eyes as the wind picked up, roaring and whistling beyond her safe place in the rock, and then as suddenly as it had appeared, it was gone.

Bree staggered out from between the rocks. "I made it." There was no sign of the four-wheel drive, not so much as tire tracks in the red dust.

Bree threw her arms skyward—an involuntary stretch in wide-open space as she sucked in lungs full of clean, warm air. The sun leaned toward the horizon. She had an hour, if that, and had to find her way back to the campsite. A night in the Australian bush in the wide-open spaces was not on her itinerary. The cool entrance of the chasm enticed her, but she wouldn't sleep with a snake for company. The sun glinted off metal, a sign at knee height.

CURDIMURKA ROCK CARVINGS AND PAINTINGS
PLEASE NO PHOTOGRAPHS—TAKE ONLY
MEMORIES AND THE STORY OF THE ARTIST
WITH YOU.

She wiped the sweat from her brow as she surveyed the terrain. Five hundred yards away, next to where the ground dipped away, a familiar landmark rose into the air. A tall, knobby skyscraper of dirt, home to ants.

Bree headed toward it, a spring in her step—a spring that hadn't been there for some time, powered by her un-explainable escape. Her feet caught in the low grass and she stumbled her way back to the crater, stepping over fresh tire tracks in the dirt. How could she approach the people who had left her stuck in a ravine with only herself to get out?

She caught herself smiling—her voice would be strong, not the tiny voice at the foot of the ravine wall.

The sun warmed her back as she stood at the crater's lip.

Bree broke down in relief. "Lize! Lincoln!" She stumbled down the soft sand wall of the crater and threw open the lid to the supply box. She gulped some tepid water and ripped open protein bars, which sat heavy and salty in her mouth as she surveyed the campsite. There were gaps in the campsite—three swags were gone, missing spokes in a broken wheel. And she heard the crunch of footsteps coming from beyond the crater.

"Lize? I made it back."

Sloaney threw his head back at the sight of her. "Oh thank goodness." He surfed down the sandy wall and rushed to her. He held her shoulders in a tight grip as he inspected her for damage. "Are you okay? Where have you been?"

She started with a deep breath. "I woke up in a ravine about five hundred yards that way, and there were snakes and some cave paintings." She looked back into Sloaney's incredulous face.

"We've been coming to this campsite for years, and I know every bump on the landscape around here. There is no ravine within fifty kilometers of here."

"But the riverbed was—"

Sloaney shook his head. "No rivers around here—that's one reason we picked it for a campsite."

Bree scanned the campsite. "Where is everyone?"

"You all disappeared the morning after the sandstorm. When the sun rose, you all were gone—all four of you and your swags."

Bree looked over her shoulder. "Three swags are missing."

Sloaney scratched his head as he pushed his hat up from his greasy blond locks. "I could have sworn four were missing . . . So where were you all day?"

"Where was I? I told you—I was in a ravine. I thought you guys did it as some kind of journey of discovery or whatever you called it." She looked up into Sloaney's slack-jawed stare.

Sloaney shook his head. "But there's nothing out there!"

"But I climbed out of the ravine and walked over a half mile to get back—"

Sloaney again gripped her shoulders and spoke slowly into her face. "There is nothing around here for kilometers."

Bree frowned. "But there was a sign for the Curdimurka Rock Carvings."

Sloaney's grip relaxed. "Curdimurka is eighty k's away."

Bree's head swam again as she held up her finger to show him the wound. "But I climbed up to the cave, and the music played, and there were berries that you left behind for me—"

Sloaney folded his arms, tight-lipped, as his eyes narrowed. "We didn't leave anything of the sort for you. If you found anything out there, it wasn't from us."

TWENTY-NINE

Lincoln pushed through the dust as it drifted to the floorboards of the stationmaster's office. "Alinta!" He burst through the front door and was washed in the twilight.

The platform was empty.

Beyond the tracks the railway signal lit green. Lincoln leaped from the platform, his ankles sinking into the soft red powder between the tracks as he scanned the railway line for her. Nothing but wavy steel reaching into the dark in each direction. But the buffer stop blocking the line was now gone.

Lincoln blinked hard into the thickening dusk as a setting sliver of gold brushed the faint gray sky into purple. The world was silent, save the dueling calls of the shift change of the Australian outback—birdlife retiring for the evening and saying farewell to those working the night shift.

The silence was all but absolute, and Lincoln absorbed

the moment. Alinta. A forgotten ring. And a sense of difference, a lightness almost. The silence cracked open with a distant noise. Lincoln threw back his head as a roar grew, and it didn't sound like the wind. He peered under the platform and saw a thick dust cloud.

A vehicle.

Lincoln clambered back onto the platform and rushed through the railway station, leaping from the platform onto the dirt road, waving his arms in a frantic attempt for attention.

The headlights on the vehicle flashed, and Lincoln dropped to his knees. His breath rushed from his throat in rasps as the black four-wheel drive grew in his vision. Alinta had come back for him, and he would see her again. He was saved, and he was about to go back.

Go back.

Back to his friends—their last conversation had not gone well—and beyond that a return home to a looming conversation that could cost him half of everything he owned, perhaps more. But the dread he expected wasn't there. The feeling was not one of acceptance but readiness to deal with things in a new light. To start this new part of his journey from a different place. To veer around this bend in life's road and take on a new horizon. He closed his eyes as he took it all in, and breathed in something new. A sense of responsibility. Of making things right. Of being better.

He got to his feet in the growing spotlights of the Outback

Tours four-wheel drive, which skidded to a halt in front of him. Lincoln smiled as the door flung open and Eddie jumped out, exasperated relief etched into his face. "Where on earth have you been, mate?" He threw him a canteen. "And how on earth did you end up *this* far away from the campsite?"

Lincoln unscrewed the canteen lid with trembling fingers and emptied it, the cold water cascading down his face as much as his throat. "What do you mean *this* far away from the campsite?"

"Curdimurka is eighty k's away from our camp."

Lincoln reeled. "So? Isn't this where you dropped me off?"

Eddie shook his head furiously. "Nah, mate. After the sandstorm broke on first light, we went to check on you to make sure you were okay, but you were gone. We thought you'd tried to find shelter in the four-wheel drive, but there was no sign of you at all. Any of you. Even your swags had gone."

"What? I woke up here. You had to have dropped me into that railway station to start this survivor thing you had us do."

Eddie breathed hard, as if reining in rising fury. "I've said all along that we're not doing anything like that. If we were, we certainly wouldn't drop you this far away and leave you to it."

Something about his anger portrayed an honesty. But it was an honesty that answered no questions. Lincoln looked past Eddie into the four-wheel drive, expecting to see Alinta's shy smile lighting up the passenger seat. But the car was empty. "I woke up here and met this woman—"

Eddie eyed him with suspicion as he reached for his satellite phone. "I've found one . . . No, Curdimurka . . . I don't know either. He says he woke up here . . . No, really . . . I'll bring him back . . . Any sign of the others?"

Others? "Isn't everyone else back at the camp?"

Eddie charged back to the four-wheel drive. "No. Get in."

Lincoln reeled. "But I've spent all day with Alinta—"

"Who?"

"She said she was a guide. I presumed she was part of this adventure you put me on."

Eddie shook his head fiercely. "We don't employ anyone else. It's me and Sloaney. And now you've got me worried that someone is out here pretending that they represent Outback Tours."

How could he explain this? He shoved his hands into his pockets and his fingers found a small, hard box that would prove his story. He fingered it, proof that he'd had a conversation with a young woman about getting over relationships of the past to free up the blockage of the future. A young woman who could retrieve items from his past and bring them into his present, who had disappeared in a sandstorm that was over almost before it had begun. Like the one at the campsite.

Lincoln pulled his hands from his pockets. He wouldn't have believed him either.

THIRTY

The truck roared its angry displeasure as Grace threw her weight behind the wheel to ease tons of metal around a tight, soft corner.

"Is that it? I had to turn right?"

"No. But would you have known which direction to go with the map you were holding?"

Eliza took one last look at the still-empty compass. Labels popped up on the map, labels with unknown words, unknown meanings. Branches that led to the map's edges and beyond. Exciting bends. Tight contours indicating the challenge of hills to climb, mountains to conquer.

Eliza shook her head. "Who *are* you?"

Grace tipped the visor of her cap. "I'm Grace." The truck roared as it swept through the gears.

"Where are we?"

Grace jerked her head across the plains to their left. "Back on track. Your campsite is over there."

The setting sun washed the outback in deep orange and pink, a featureless landscape except one tall, knobbly construction that pointed into the fiery heavens.

A dirt skyscraper, built by ants.

Eliza's eyes moistened as her lip quivered. She choked back a sob, before dissolving into long-overdue tears. "What can I say? I'm grateful—thankful—for your perspective and for your help."

Grace's lips parted in a broad smile. "You're welcome. That's what I'm supposed to do. You take that map with you. I think it's now far more useful than it was."

Eliza folded up the paper sprawled across her lap and slipped it into her backpack. She opened the heavy door and swung it open. "There is someone I want you to meet. Bree, my friend, could really benefit from your perspective and working out how she should progress in her life."

Grace's ponytail shook. "This is as far as I can come, and you might find Bree needed something else."

Eliza lunged across the cabin, enveloping Grace with a tight hug. Gratitude flooded through her. "Would you at least come and meet her?"

Grace smiled to herself, almost as if enjoying a secret memory. "No, this is my limit." She tapped papers held up under the sun visor. "I've got a schedule to keep."

The businesswoman in Eliza recognized the professionalism and logistics, but she couldn't sever this connection so easily. "Well, do you have a card or something? An email address? Give me your cell."

Grace nodded to Eliza's backpack. "Check the map."

With a nod, Eliza jumped from the cabin, the gravel crunching under her landing. She hefted the backpack onto her shoulder. The wind picked up as the rumbling road train crawled away, grinding to higher gears that pushed it, thundering, into the gloom.

Eliza shielded her eyes as the growing wind flung dust and dirt at her, before with one final roar it dropped as suddenly as it appeared. Eliza spun—the truck was gone, taking with it a woman with insights. And while she didn't subscribe to much she couldn't prove, she certainly couldn't justify her experience. She only knew it was real.

The sunlight bathed the outback for her third day in Australia, and she broke into a jog toward the crater and the campsite. She had a story to tell. Grace's comment flitted back into her thinking.

Bree needed something else? What had happened to Bree?

Eliza hitched her backpack higher on her shoulders and her jog graduated into a sprint.

She heard voices ahead. Two of them. She wasn't the first one back. That didn't seem to matter now.

Eliza climbed the lip of the crater, preparing to face a triumphant Lincoln and whatever he was going to throw at her. Neither of the voices belonged to Lincoln. Sloaney stood in animated discussion with Bree.

"Breezy!" Eliza rushed down the crater, half-stumbling down the soft sides of their campsite. Bree rushed toward her, arms outstretched, and they dissolved into a sobbing hug.

Their stories flowed over each other as Eliza gripped Bree by the shoulders. "You won't believe what happened to me."

Bree wiped away tears. "I was going to say the same thing to you. I've had this amazing experience I can't believe actually happened." And as she started her story—of a ravine Sloaney said didn't exist—the gravity of it settled on Eliza. She wasn't the only one with an experience that was all but impossible.

Sloaney ran up to them. "Eliza! Where have you been?"

"I woke up where you left me by the dirt track."

Sloaney's blank face gave no hint of guilt. "Left you? We didn't leave you anywhere. What type of tour group do you think we are?"

"How else could I be transported in the middle of the night to the middle of nowhere? If you want proof of it, we need to find that dirt track where my swag is, the place where Grace picked me up—"

"Who is Grace?" Sloaney ran his hand through his grubby blond curls.

Eliza rummaged through her backpack. "This will prove it. She gave me a map with my own face on it that showed my

271

reference point was actually myself." She frowned and dug harder into the bag. "It's not here. You both heard the road train that brought me back, didn't you?"

Bree and Sloaney both shook their heads.

Flushed, Eliza turned on Sloaney and jabbed a finger in the air. "You put us through this journey of discovery thing with no preparation at all." She pointed at the campsite. "And how did you get my swag back from my journey?"

Sloaney's head scratching continued. "What journey?"

Eliza stopped her friend as she stomped toward the campsite. "How long did it take Lincoln and Andy to get back?"

Sloaney appeared, offering her a canteen. "They're not here."

Eliza froze. "So where are they?"

A long fissure ripped its way through Sloaney's laid-back facade, cracking his voice. "We don't know, okay? They disappeared like you two did."

THIRTY-ONE

B ree rose on the balls of her feet, as if inflated with something new. An empowering indignation. A platform for
her courage. She rounded on Sloaney with a pointed finger.
"Hang on a minute. If we were to disappear, don't you think
we would have taken the car?"

"We didn't know—"

Eliza advanced on him. "What do you mean they're not
back?"

Sloaney's voice cracked as if struggling to maintain a
pace it was unused to. "Their swags are gone, just like yours."

Bree looked beyond Sloaney to the tents spaced around
the campfire. She counted in her head, frowned, and counted
again. "There are only two swags missing."

Sloaney and Eliza turned to the campfire. Only two gaps
remained in the spacing among the tents; one had been replaced by a neat pile of stacked rocks. A pocket game of God's
Jenga.

Bree zeroed in on Sloaney. "What's going on? You play this trick on me by leaving me in a ravine—"

Eliza stepped forward. "I thought it was a spiritual trek or journey or whatever you're calling it—"

Sloaney pushed up his hat and scratched at the curls that sprung free as his gaze swung back to the unfinished circle of tents. "How did that swag appear? And where did those stones come from?"

Bree turned to Eliza. "This is real, Lize. I know I was in a ravine. I know I scaled the wall to get out, and I got past the snake to make a break for freedom. I overcame my fears and I know it was real."

Sloaney's head continued to shake. "But there isn't a ravine within a hundred k's of here."

Bree pulled back her sleeve. "How did I get this then?" She held her hand up in the fading twilight. A thick cut lined with congealed blood sliced her hand. "If this whole journey was in my head, the scars it left are real."

Sloaney's mouth flapped as a silence crept across the crater. Three minds churned to find elusive answers to pressing questions. The silence was shattered by the crunch of gravel and the roar of an engine.

Bree raced toward the crater's edge. "The guys are back." The memory of her last climb made scaling the crater wall feel like a short scramble up a gentle incline. Eliza rose to her feet, Sloaney hot on her heels, as the Outback Tours four-wheel drive arrived.

The driver's door flung open and Eddie jumped out. "So how many do we have back?"

Sloaney jerked his head back into the crater, as Eliza appeared at its lip. "Two now."

The passenger door eased open and two feet were placed gently on the ground. Lincoln stood to his full height and Bree rushed toward him.

Sloaney charged toward Eddie. "How did he get to Curdimurka?"

Eddie brushed past him and stormed up to Bree and Eliza. "Where have you two been?"

Lincoln pushed past him to embrace them. "You won't believe what happened to me—"

Bree smiled at Eliza. "Try us."

Eddie thrust his hands onto his hips, his voice shaking. "Where in the heck have you been—?"

Eliza stepped forward and pointed a finger into Eddie's chest. "You listen to me. This walkabout thing, or whatever you want to call it that you organized, nearly killed me. I almost died out there of dehydration. If I hadn't been found by the road train driver—"

Eddie stared at her, a seething anger surfing under his voice. "There was no such thing. As I said to you all along, it's not appropriate to exploit cultural heritage for tourists."

Sloaney stepped forward. "After the sandstorm passed, we checked on you in the middle of the night, but you were all gone. We thought you'd been disoriented and had wandered off looking for shelter. We've been searching for you all day."

Eddie glanced at the crater. "Your swags were all gone. I see you've brought yours back though."

Eliza stared intensely at Lincoln's wrist, her voice emerging in a monotone. "Mine was left by the side of the road."

Bree counted the swags surrounding the campfire. "Now only one is missing. It should be where that pile of rocks is." She drifted her gaze to the four-wheel drive. "So where's Andy?"

The wind picked up, the tiniest chill on the growing breeze. Distant lightning crept closer, driven by the blanket of thick, dark clouds.

Their friend was still out there.

THIRTY-TWO

His fingers laced together, Lincoln fidgeted as he sat at the cold gray table of the police station in the middle of the country, his thumbs chasing each other in an endless loop. Eliza's fingernails beat a steady tattoo, while Bree's nails were already halfway bitten.

The sheen had well and truly worn off their reunion.

It had been a long three hours since the police car ride back into town—exhausting interviews conducted by disbelieving detectives. Their stories—which they each thought to be unbelievable—were a variation of another's. Except Andy's, which remained untold.

Lincoln swallowed hard. "I still don't know what happened. One minute I'm diving into my swag in the middle of a sandstorm, the next minute I'm awake in a train station."

Eliza shrugged. "Same story, but dirt road for me."

Bree shook her head in disbelieving wonder. "At least

you two didn't have to run from a snake. So what on earth happened?"

Eliza shook her head. "I don't know. All I know is that I met a wonderful young woman who saved my life in more ways than one."

"Me too." Lincoln laughed bitterly as the phrase he regularly derided became a part of his story.

Lincoln could see Bree was itching to add to the conversation, but she was holding back. He urged her to speak. "So who did you meet?"

"You wouldn't believe me if I told you."

"Based on what we've been through in the past forty-eight hours?"

"Okay." Bree took a deep breath as tears formed in the corners of her eyes. "When I climbed out of the ravine, away from the snake, I reached a cave and in there were paintings that gave me instructions to overcome my fear, to tame a venomous snake, and get out." Her gaze dropped to the carpet.

Eliza reached across and set a hand on Bree's arm. "For me it was a map with my own life printed on it. I can't even begin to explain it, but I'll never forget Grace's simple question about why I was the reference point for my own life. I was saved by Grace."

Lincoln was quiet, buried in his own thoughts.

Bree leaned across to him. "What did you take away from all this?"

Lincoln's cheeks burned with a sheepish embarrassment. "The woman I met showed me how I had locked away rejection of the past that was hindering all other relationships."

Eliza averted her eyes, but only as far as his wrist. "You've still got that from the trip to Africa?"

Lincoln fingered the simple woven string around his wrist and shrugged. "I guess so." Eliza smiled at him and, in that moment, the tiniest spark flared. "I left a part of myself behind back then, but I think I need to get that part of the old me back."

Eliza's smile didn't seem forced. "You know, I was on that straight stretch of road for hours, and it wasn't until I made the decision to step out of the driver's seat of my own life that I found my way back." She laced her hands behind her head. "So what do we do? Clearly the police here think we did something, but they didn't believe my story."

Two heads shook around the table as Lincoln and Bree answered in unison. "Me neither."

Distant footsteps approached them down the corridor before they stopped outside the door.

Three heads pivoted to the door and Lincoln threw back his head in relief. "That has to be Andy. What do you think happened to him on his journey?"

EPILOGUE

Andy cracked one eye open as his consciousness reluctantly returned in the warming air. A sea of red. Blood? His nose filled with swirling puffs of acrid, white-hot dust, pluming in the air from each labored breath. Ancient, jagged rocks cut into his cheek. Leaden arms glued to the ground, the weight of his past pinning him to the hot dust of Central Australia.

Red.

Red dust.

The realization of where he was landed on him with a thud. He wished he'd never remembered. His mind was running. It had been running all night. He shook his consciousness back into shape and peeked out from his safe crevice in the ancient rock to see if the noises that had tormented his night had an owner. His stomach growled in impatient frustration, a sentient being of its own, unfulfilled after the tiniest sliver of pizza.

Andy craned his neck outside the cave and looked up, beyond the outcrop, into the brightness of the morning. A shadow flitted in the red dirt in front of him. He couldn't keep going like this. He'd been running for years, lessons unlearned, consequences piling up like uncanceled junk mail on a vacationer's front door step.

Smithy's faint voice echoed in his head. *"I am prepared to pay your debt. That's all I've prepared for."*

Instead, Andy had run.

He reached for his phone. The battery was clinging to life by its fingertips, but the phone was no closer to a signal. He dropped it as it buzzed in his hand. Andy bent to pick it up from the rock beneath his feet and turned it over.

The message wasn't from his bookie. Beneath the spider-webbed glass the sender's name was clear: the Front Bar. Andy fumbled the phone as he switched it off.

"I am prepared to pay your debt."

With the echo of Smithy's soothing voice, his heart rate slowed. He forced his entire being into his feet, driving them to twitch, to get him upright and back to Smithy. One chance to turn things around and he'd blown it.

He had to find Smithy again, but he had no idea how. The one person who had offered to stand up for him, stand alongside him as he fought the twinges to put his future on the line for a rush in the present, and stand for the price that needed to be paid to free him.

"I am not far away."

The last time Andy had stumbled across him under a gum tree. As he scanned the landscape between himself and the horizon, there were only a handful of options.

Anxiety rose in him like a flood at the thought of the barman chasing him for money. As if by reflex, layered with panic and years of survival, he kicked into gear. He emerged from under the rock as the burning sun hit him, crisping his shoulders as he left his hiding place.

The phone buzzed again.

And he ran.

A NOTE FROM THE AUTHOR

Dear Friend,

Thank you for investing your time in reading this story. I hope you enjoyed it and the brief visit to my country.

As much as the corner of the Outback in which my American characters found themselves was fictional, it was representative of the wonder and rugged, harsh beauty of the heart of Australia. Come and visit—there will be no lack of ravines, sweeping dunes, abandoned railways or dirt tracks for you to enjoy, lose yourself and—hopefully—find yourself.

I really wanted to write a story about Australia. It's a rugged, dangerous, enchanting place, and I wanted to share it with you. If you ever get a chance to visit Australia, I'd highly recommend it. When you're in the outback, you really are in the middle of nowhere, standing on the crushed red dust of the heart of this land, and you can hear your thoughts before you even have them. It's beautiful.

The other thing about being in the middle of nowhere is it gives you a chance to reflect. To think. To ask the question: How did I get here? You may have even thought about that yourself. I know I have.

It's a question we'd all do well to at least ask. We might find that the path we're on isn't the right one, but asking that question early enough gives us time to rethink and reshape. Or we might find that the path we thought we'd be on—the path we knew was best for us—wasn't actually the way we should have gone.

So that became the theme of the book: How did I get here? My stories always come with a theme. With *The Baggage Handler*, the story was about dealing with emotional baggage. With *The Camera Never Lies*, the theme was about the price of accepting honesty with others and our-selves.

So with the theme for this book, I'd like to pose that question to you: How did you get to where you are? Are you like Eliza, unsure of the value of your life because you've been at the center of it? Or perhaps like Bree—held back by fear and avoiding the opportunities that arise. Maybe Lincoln—held back by locking part of yourself away and the rest of the world out. Or even Andy, who is still running from the mess he's created.

If you'd like to explore this further, I have some starter questions on the next page. I don't do this to give you homework—but it will continue the thought process of not only working out how you got here but also where you might go from this place in your life. Around the bend in the road, to face whatever's next.

Take care,

David.

DISCUSSION QUESTIONS

1. How did you get to the point you are at in life?
2. Is there a particular character you related to, in terms of where they were at in life?
3. Is there a particular character whose challenges you related to? Who, and why?
4. If you connected with more than one character, which parts of them spoke to you?
5. Each of the characters had a guide to bring them to the next phase of their life's journey. Who around you could fill that role for you, or who would you like to play that role?
6. If you could stop at this juncture of your life and head in any direction at all, in which direction would you go?
7. What has shaped your life's journey?
8. Are there events from your past—actions by other

people, yourself, circumstance, or even the worst of luck—that have put you on your current trajectory?

9. Where is this trajectory taking you?

10. Like Bree, are there voices from your past that convince you that you are unable to overcome challenges? If so, how are you able to address them?

11. Bree was faced with fear stopping her from even attempting things outside her comfort zone. How would you address this?

12. Why would Bree keep a secret like the New York audition from Eliza over the years? If you were either Bree or Eliza in that situation, what would you do?

13. Like Lincoln, are there people in your past whose actions have driven you away from the person you are meant to be?

14. Lincoln covered the pain of rejection with materialism. How would you handle that if a friend was living that life?

15. Ultimately, Andy decided that it was easier to run than face up to the consequences of his actions. How long do you think Andy will be running for? What would it take for him to stop running?

16. Eliza said she had moved on, fifteen years after breaking up with Lincoln. What did you think of that—is that fair?

17. Lincoln was still, in his own way, clinging to the past. Should he have moved on? If so, how? If not, why not?

18. Whose face is in the center of your life's compass?

19. What do you think the sandstorm represented? And the wind that carried away certain guides? Were there any other symbolic elements of the Australian outback that represented parts of the characters' journeys?

20. Like Andy, do you entertain compulsions in your life you know are unhealthy for you?

ACKNOWLEDGMENTS

To God: thank You for the lessons along the way that make all this possible.

To my family, as always, for believing these stories are worth telling and I am worth supporting. And I'm glad you enjoyed our outback research holiday.

To the usual suspects of my support crew: James L. Rubart, a mentor who not only leads from the front but is also behind with support; Steve Laube, an agent with integrity; my parents, for their continued enthusiasm; the Fulwood family, for having my creative back; and my family at Edwardstown Baptist, particularly those in the life group who have heard the twists and turns of a new author's first steps. Special thanks to Deanne Hanchant-Nichols from the University of South Australia; Haydyn Bromley from the Aboriginal Lands Trust; and Allan Sumner, a gifted artist from the Aboriginal Cultural Arts Centre Aldinga, for helping continue my understanding of and deepening my respect for our First Nations people.

To the team at HarperCollins Christian Publishing: Becky Monds, my wonderful editorial director, for helping me find the story within the story, and the wonderful team members across editorial, marketing, and sales, but particularly Paul Fisher, Allison Carter, Laura Wheeler, Brittany Lassiter, Margaret Kercher, Amanda Bostic, and Halie Cotton, designer of great covers. I couldn't do this without you, not from this side of the planet. And to Julee Schwarzburg, for her razor-sharp story observations and her contribution of translating this story into my second language of American English.

To the land of Australia. My home. A wonderful, exotic, dangerous, gorgeous land that as a backdrop for a novel is all but impossible to do justice to with the written word.

All characters in this work are fictitious. Resemblance to real persons, living or dead, is purely coincidental, although if you see yourself in these pages, maybe someone's trying to tell you something.

If you'd like to know when
my next book is coming out,
please sign up for my newsletter
or read some excerpts on my website. You might also enjoy some
short stories while you're there.

www.davidrawlings.com.au

2019 Christy Award Winner

In a similar vein to *The Traveler's Gift* by Andy Andrews or *Dinner with a Perfect Stranger* by David Gregory, *The Baggage Handler* is a contemporary story that explores one question:

What baggage are you carrying?